Why was Emma hiding her face? Travis wondered.

He ran his right arm along the back of the seat until he was close enough to grab the fabric at the back of her hood.

One quick yank was all it took to uncover her head.

She was startled, of course, but that was not what caught and held his attention.

Her hair was wild and tangled, as if she hadn't brushed it in days. Her blue eyes were swimming. Worst of all, there was an angry-looking black-and-blue mark on her cheek. It was strong and dark, fresh rather than fading, and the sight of it tied his gut in a knot.

"Emma! Who did that to you?"

As she turned toward him more fully, tears tipped over her lower lashes and began to slide silently down her chapped, bruised cheeks.

He could tell she was struggling to speak. Lifting his hand slowly, deliberately, he reached toward her and wiped away a tear with one finger, barely touching her as he did so.

Who had hurt her? And why?

Books by Valerie Hansen

Love Inspired Suspense

*Her Brother's Keeper
*Out of the Depths
 Deadly Payoff
*Shadow of Turning
 Hidden in the Wall
*Nowhere to Run
*No Alibi
*My Deadly Valentine
   "Dangerous Admirer"
 Face of Danger
†Nightwatch
 The Rookie's Assignment
†Threat of Darkness
†Standing Guard
 Explosive Secrets
 Family in Hiding
†A Trace of Memory

Love Inspired Historical

 Frontier Courtship
 Wilderness Courtship
 High Plains Bride
 The Doctor's Newfound Family
 Rescuing the Heiress

Love Inspired

*The Perfect Couple
*Second Chances
*Love One Another
*Blessings of the Heart
*Samantha's Gift
*Everlasting Love
 The Hamilton Heir
*A Treasure of the Heart
 Healing the Boss's Heart
 Cozy Christmas
 Her Montana Cowboy

*Serenity, Arkansas
†The Defenders

VALERIE HANSEN

was thirty when she awoke to the presence of the Lord in her life and turned to Jesus. In the years that followed, she worked with young children, both in church and secular environments. She also raised a family of her own and played foster mother to a wide assortment of furred and feathered critters.

She loves to hike the wooded hills behind her house and reflect on the marvelous turn her life has taken. Not only is she privileged to reside among the loving, accepting folks in the breathtakingly beautiful Ozark mountains of Arkansas, she also gets to share her personal faith by telling the stories of her heart in Love Inspired Books.

Life doesn't get much better than that!

A TRACE
OF MEMORY

VALERIE HANSEN

HARLEQUIN® LOVE INSPIRED® SUSPENSE

Recycling programs
for this product may
not exist in your area.

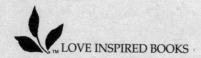

™ LOVE INSPIRED BOOKS

ISBN-13: 978-0-373-44613-1

A TRACE OF MEMORY

Copyright © 2014 by Valerie Whisenand

www.Harlequin.com

Printed in U.S.A.

The Lord hears good people when they cry out to Him,
and He saves them from all their troubles.
—*Psalms* 34:17

To my Joe, who will always be
looking over my shoulder as I write.
He was an extraordinary gift from God.

ONE

Run! Run! He's coming!

Emma Landers heard her own frantic, breathless screams echoing in the dark hallway. Clawing her way around a corner, hands palming the bare walls, she saw a dim outline to her left. A door? Had her prayers been answered?

She flew against it, her fingers raking the cold, metal surface like the talons of a trapped bird of prey.

Quick, heavy footfalls echoed behind her. It didn't matter who her pursuer was, she somehow knew she must elude him. At all costs.

Her trembling fingers closed around the doorknob. Tried to twist it and failed. Slipped. Hurt.

"No, no, no," Emma rasped. "It can't be locked." Tendrils of her sandy-blond hair clung to the perspiration dotting her forehead and she felt droplets slithering down her spine.

Someone began shouting in the distance. Who? Why? And why was she so frightened she could hardly breathe let alone function capably?

Unfortunately, she didn't remember much of anything prior to this terrifying moment. The only fact that was solid in her mind was the desperate need to escape, to put miles between herself and whoever or whatever was rapidly closing in.

Hoping to find a key hanging nearby, she left the door to explore the nearby walls of her prison, acting like a mime trapped in an invisible box. Dust coated everything, clinging to her clammy hands and clogging her already tight throat.

An uneven place on the floor caught her attention. Crouching in the darkness, she located a small grit-and-mud-covered mat next to the doorway and recoiled.

Fingertips of one hand resting lightly on the floor for balance, she racked her foggy brain. What were the chances of finding a key under that filthy rug? Slim to none. But there was only one way to find out for sure.

Emma located an edge by feel, tossed the mat aside and began frantically searching the slick, hard floor. There was something there, all right. Something flat and small with distinct edges. *Praise the Lord!*

If she hadn't been shaking so badly she might have been able to fit the key into the slot in the center of the knob without delay. Instead, she fumbled the precious metal object and nearly dropped it several times before it finally slid into place.

Twisting with all her might, Emma heard the lock's tumblers click. The knob turned. Freedom!

Where she was didn't matter. Where she would go once she left this building or what she might face on the outside didn't, either. Not really. At least not yet.

She jerked the door toward her on squeaking hinges.

Cold, damp air enveloped her. It was night, and she was staring into the forbidding depths of a forest that lay just beyond a paved parking area.

A man's coarse voice called, "You're smarter than I thought you were, Emma darlin'. Stop running. That's not the way to win me over."

His words weren't all that gave her feet wings. It was the way his menacing tone made her bones ache and her heart pound that spurred her to break and run.

She never looked back. Not even when he threatened her again and began to fire a gun.

One of the bullets hit a nearby tree with a dull thunk and rained bits of bark down as she dodged several parked pickup trucks and plunged into the thick underbrush beyond.

Emma wasn't going to stop just because her enemy was armed. She was finally free. That was all that mattered.

Branches tore at her flimsy T-shirt and scratched her cheeks, although she tried to push the foliage aside as she plunged deeper into the woods. Every breath hurt. Her stomach cramped and there was a stitch in her side that nearly doubled her over.

In her wake, she could hear more shouting, as if her original pursuer had been joined by several others. Whoever they were, their foul cursing told her she'd better not slow down. Not if she wanted to live.

The fact that the shooting had stopped was a good sign. It probably meant they could no longer see her. It also meant that she had less of an idea how close they were or whether they may have fanned out in an attempt to surround her or cut her off.

That frightening thought provided enough incentive to keep her going. She didn't stop until her headlong dash brought her to a two-lane highway. Resting, bent over with her hands on her knees for support, she fought to catch her breath and assess her situation.

There wasn't much passing traffic. Emma suspected her enemies might have doubled back to continue their chase via one of the vehicles she'd noticed during her escape. Therefore, she decided to concentrate on flagging down the least likely conveyance to pose a danger—a long-haul semi.

Her shirt was bright white, her hair blond, giving her a fair chance of being noticed if she stepped onto the roadway.

Without taking time to consider the danger of doing so, she scrambled over the shoulder at the side of the slow lane and began to wave her arms above her head, praying a friendly trucker would stop before someone else showed up to grab her.

Two big rigs sailed past. The brakes of the third squealed and brought the semi to a halt as it passed her and eased partway off the road.

Emma was running toward it before it had fully stopped. She jumped onto the outside step, grabbed the door handle and threw herself inside where she collapsed, shoulders on the seat, knees on the floor of the cab.

"Drive! Please," she wheezed at the trucker. "Get me out of here!"

Travis Wright had done well at the weekly cattle auction in Serenity. The four yearlings he'd brought to the sale barn had sold for top dollar. He picked up his check from the cashier, stuck it in his wallet and fished his keys out of his jeans pocket as he headed for his farm truck and empty stock trailer.

The setting sun glinted off the windshield, obscuring the interior of the cab. As Travis circled to the driver's side he noted movement.

Jerking open the door, he was prepared to scold whoever had invaded his space. The only sound that came out of his mouth, however, was a startled gasp.

His jaw dropped. His brown eyes widened. His heartbeat increased. The frail-looking figure cowering on the passenger side was a mere shadow of her former beauty, but he would have recognized her anywhere.

She didn't smile. Didn't even blink. A gray hood from her sweatshirt was pulled over her head, nearly obscuring her usually satiny hair, and the hands that clutched the hood close beneath her chin were thin, trembling and covered with nasty-looking scratches.

Travis found his voice. "Emma?"

She nodded.

"Where did you come from?"

Her lips parted momentarily before she bit the lower one and mutely shook her head.

"What's wrong? Are you sick? Do you need a doctor?"

Again, she shook her head.

Her appearance was so tragic he could only imagine that she had been traumatized and had to restrain himself from reaching for her. "Do you want me to call the police?"

Emma finally managed to speak. "No police. Just take me home."

"Home? Your mother sold everything and left town after your dad died."

His heart was already racing. When Emma said, "Take me home with you," it nearly beat its way out of his chest.

The closer they got to the Serenity square, the more Emma started to recall about her past. Yes, there were differences in the town but much was unchanged. At least she thought so. Given her lingering feelings of confusion, nothing was certain, least of all fleeting memories.

The denim-clad man who had greeted her with such surprise was the most familiar of all. Clearly he knew her. And he knew where she had once lived. That would be very helpful, particularly if she could get him to fill her in without revealing how little she, herself, recalled, including his full name.

The logo on the truck had said Wright Ranch and she had recognized it immediately, so she assumed his last name was Wright. As for his first name, it kept dancing around the edges of her mind like a will-o'-the-wisp. It was on the tip of her tongue, so close she felt almost able to say it, yet so obscure she feared she might make a mistake if she tried.

For some reason, she kept thinking that hiding her illness, or whatever it was, would be for the best, at least until she knew more about herself. Since she had no idea who had shot at her as she'd fled, she wasn't ready to trust anybody. Not even the man seated beside her.

The hood of the sweatshirt the kind trucker had given her masked her cheeks enough that she was able to sneak a sidelong glance at this man without making it obvious. He was definitely good-looking, in a rugged sort of way. His hands, clenched on the wheel, were strong and masculine. His jaw was square. His hair—what little she could see of it sticking out from beneath the baseball cap he wore, was as dark and richly brown as his eyes.

More than that, she was getting a sense of belonging, as if she and this person had once been close. For one thing, he had recognized her. For another, his expression had been poignant, as if he cared, maybe even had missed her.

Closing her eyes, Emma let her thoughts drift. She considered praying but before she had time to begin, a name popped into her mind.

"Travis."

His head snapped around.

"Your name is Travis."

"Of course it is. And you're Emma Lynn Landers, the woman who broke my heart six years ago and ran off with a guitar-playing Romeo. What of it?"

All Emma could do was bite her lip to control her emotions. She now knew a little about her past, although it didn't sound as if she'd been a very nice person.

She took a moment to compose herself before she said, "I'm sorry, Travis. I am so, so sorry."

He huffed. "Yeah, so am I."

Ever since Emma had blurted out his name so strangely, Travis had been surreptitiously studying her. She was hunched down as if trying to make herself invisible and kept glancing in the side mirror of his truck.

"Why are you doing that, Emma?"

"Doing what?"

"Checking behind us. Is somebody after you?"

"No, I…"

"Then why are you acting so scared?"

"I guess I'm just overtired."

"Right. And I'm imagining things. Is that what you want me to believe?"

When she didn't answer, he found himself mimicking her actions and checking the road behind them. "Now you've got me seeing things. I actually do think we're being followed."

"No!" She slid lower in the seat, pulled the hood tighter. "We can't be. There's no way they could have known how I got here."

"They, who?"

"I don't know."

Travis shrugged. "Have it your way. The truck I thought was tailing us just turned off. You can sit up now."

"You said that on purpose to scare me, didn't you?"

"Actually, no." Travis had noticed a dark pickup pacing them. Since the state of Arkansas required only rear license plates, there was no way he could tell if the truck was local. "I did see someone."

"Are they gone now?"

"Apparently."

She swiveled to look behind them, seeing only the towed stock trailer. "How can you be sure? Maybe they just pulled really close so we couldn't see them anymore."

"In that case, they'll pass us if I pull over," Travis said logically.

His rig was too long to park next to the county courthouse so he continued out of town as far as the little league baseball field before easing off the road and turning to face her.

"Look at me, Emma."

She was concentrating on the passing traffic, instead, peering at it as if one of the vehicles might be carrying public enemy number one.

Travis reached to touch her arm.

She jumped at the contact.

"All right," he said, chagrined. "Why are you here and why did you come to me?"

"I was riding by, saw your truck and recognized the ranch logo."

"Riding? How?"

"In a semi. I'd been hitchhiking."

Frustrated by not being able to look directly into her eyes, Travis made a calculated decision. At this point it didn't matter whether Emma got mad at him or not. He wasn't going to let her hide her face. Not if she wanted him to take her the rest of the way to the ranch.

Keeping his left hand on the steering wheel, he ran his right arm along the back of the seat until he was close enough to grab the fabric at the back of her hood.

One quick yank was all it took to uncover her head.

She was startled, of course, but that was not what caught and held his attention.

Her hair was wild and tangled, as if she hadn't brushed it in days. Her blue eyes were swimming. Worst of all, there was an angry-looking bruise on her cheek. It was strong and dark, fresh rather than fading, and the sight of it tied his gut in a knot.

"Emma! Who did that to you?"

As she turned toward him more fully, tears tipped over her lower lashes and began to slide silently down her chapped, bruised cheeks.

He could tell she was struggling to speak. Lifting his hand slowly, deliberately, he reached toward her and wiped away a tear with one finger, barely touching her as he did so.

To his surprise, Emma grasped his hand, pulled his palm against her cheek and laid her head against it as if begging him to cradle her injuries.

Travis was glad they were both restricted by their seat belts because if they had not been, he was afraid he might have dragged her into his arms at that moment despite their rocky past.

Someone had hurt his Emma. And as soon as she told him who was responsible, he was going to see that justice was done. One way or the other.

TWO

Emma would have gladly told this kind man anything he wanted to know, if she'd been able. But she wasn't.

She bravely met his gaze, willing him to understand without having to spell it out. It was too soon to admit she was emotionally or mentally impaired—or whatever was wrong with her. There were instances when she felt back in control, yet, more often than not, she found herself floundering as if she were a little lost child.

This was one such instance. Smiling, she sniffled and swiped at her tears before she said, "I've been on the road for at least twenty-four hours and I'm worn out. Can we please just go home?"

"You really want me to take you to my place?"

Emma nodded. She couldn't have explained her trust in Travis if her life had depended upon it, which it very well might. She simply knew that this man would not hurt her the way others had. That was enough.

"Yes. Please," she said softly.

"All right." Straightening, he put the truck in gear and pulled back onto the roadway. The tension between them was palpable. She could tell he was upset, if not actually angry. And, if she really had jilted him in the past, she could understand why.

He—*Travis,* she reminded herself—seemed like a caring person. One in whom she could safely confide. If nothing happened to change her mind she would eventually tell him all she knew. And maybe, by that time, there would be more to tell. She certainly hoped so because being in limbo, the way she currently was, was not how she intended to spend the rest of her life.

However long that might be, Emma added, trembling. She felt relatively safe at the moment, but that was no guarantee that whoever had kept her prisoner and had shot at her as she'd run into the woods was no longer looking for her.

How will I know my enemies?

That question made her shudder and check the mirror again. The traffic behind the stock trailer looked innocent enough, but…

Icy fingers of fear crept up her spine and spread along every nerve. How could she possibly protect herself when she didn't even know who had hurt her? Or why. If she had treated a nice guy like Travis badly, as he claimed, what was to say she had not done other terrible things?

Emma chanced a sidelong glance at him and caught him watching her. Judging by his expression he was less angry than he was puzzled. That made two of them.

"You probably think I'm acting very strange."

His eyebrows arched. "Lady, that is the biggest understatement I've heard in years."

"It's complicated."

"Undoubtedly. Well, we're almost there, as you can see," Travis said, making a turn onto a dirt road. "Maybe you'll feel more like talking to Cleo."

Searching recent memory brought only confusion. "Cleo?"

"My aunt. She stayed on with me after my dad and his brother Jim both died and I inherited the ranch. I needed help and Cleo needed a place to live where she felt useful."

"Oh. I see."

Emma closed her eyes, letting her thoughts drift. When she tried to focus on anything in the weeks prior to her flight from the locked door, dense clouds masked the memories like a fog bank lying in the bottom lands along the river on a damp Ozark morning.

The truth was there somewhere. It had to be.

All Emma had to do was wait until the mist lifted. Trouble was, she didn't know where the haziness had come from or how long it was going to last. All she could hope for was that being with Travis Wright would heal the unseen damage to her emotions.

If it did not, she didn't know how she would survive in a world filled with shadows of menace that might cost her her life.

The sight of the familiar redbrick ranch house with its white metal roof lifted Travis's spirits. It was always good to come home, even now, when he was probably bringing trouble with him.

Given Emma's current unpredictability, he was glad Cleo would be there, particularly because he was teetering on the edge of his self-control and getting far too close to making a fool of himself over Emma. Again.

He drove past the barn and parked behind the house before he honked to add to the barking welcome his four dogs were giving him. As he had hoped, the sound of the horn brought his middle-aged aunt to the door.

The salt-and-pepper-haired woman was wiping her hands on a kitchen towel as she stepped onto the porch. "What's wrong, Travis?"

"We have company." After quickly circling the truck with the pack of dogs at his heels, he opened Emma's door for her.

"Oh, my stars!" Cleo sounded ecstatic. "What a wonderful surprise."

She was down the porch steps and hurrying toward Emma in mere seconds. When she got close enough to see the girl's face, however, she stopped and stared, then looked to her nephew. "What happened?"

"Don't know. She was sitting in my truck when I finished at the auction. I have no idea where she came from or how she got there. She said she hitchhiked back to Serenity." He made a face that mirrored his frustration. "Maybe you can get her to tell you more."

"Did you call the sheriff?" Cleo asked.

Emma said her first word to the older woman then. "Don't."

"All right, honey. First we'll get you showered and into some clean clothes. Then we can have a bite to eat. You'll feel more like yourself after that."

With a sheltering arm around Emma's shoulders, Cleo guided her toward the house while Bo, an arthritic, aged bluetick hound, tagged along.

"Bring her suitcase," Cleo called back.

"There isn't one. What you see is all you get," Travis said flatly. "If you don't have any clothes that will fit her, I can make a run into town."

"I think you'd best stay here for now." His aunt shot him a look of concern before adding, "Just in case."

Travis could understand Cleo's trepidation because he shared it. Whatever was wrong with Emma was not simple; nor was it likely to pass quickly. He didn't know much about the workings of the human mind, but he'd seen plenty of animals who had never recovered from being ill-treated.

One of the mixed-breed dogs he'd rescued from the local shelter was like that. Normally, she acted just like the rest of the farm's pack, but accidentally do something that set her off and she'd start to tremble uncontrollably.

He and Cleo had never laid a hand on that dog. It didn't matter. There was a scar in the canine's mind that overrode all the kindness they had shown since they'd adopted her.

Travis covertly studied Emma as he followed the women toward the house. Emma was damaged, too. Perhaps severely. And it was going to be up to him to help her heal.

"With the Lord's help," he muttered. "I don't think I can be objective enough to do it alone."

His musings were disturbed when the three dogs that had stayed outside with him suddenly leaped off the back porch and raced around the house, barking.

Travis stiffened. The pack sounded angry, defensive rather than excited about chasing prey the way they did when one of them scented a raccoon or a possum.

Anyone who had owned dogs could tell the difference in their barks. And anybody who lived in the country knew better than to venture out unarmed when his dogs sounded an alarm like that.

Travis burst into the kitchen, startling Cleo and Emma. Only old Bo, the dog that had stayed with the women, seemed aware that something was amiss.

"Stay in here and lock the doors," Travis ordered. He reached onto the top of a kitchen cabinet for a pistol and checked that it was loaded. "I'm going to go see what's got the dogs so upset."

"Be careful," Cleo warned. "Could be a two-legged skunk." She pulled Emma closer. "Isn't that right, girl?"

The last thing Travis saw as he ducked back out the door was tears pooling in Emma's wide, blue eyes.

Emma was desperately worried about Travis. She didn't let herself be shepherded out of the kitchen and up the stairs to the second story until Cleo suggested they'd have a better view of the surrounding terrain from up there.

The older woman proceeded to a bedroom window and beckoned. "Take a look from over here."

As soon as Emma was by her side, Cleo began to point. "There's the lane you came up just now. Beyond the creek is the Hall place. A lot of their kin live hereabouts, too."

"I'm sorry. I don't remember," Emma said softly.

"That's okay. It'll come back to you."

Leaving that room, Cleo led Emma to the opposite side of the house and raised the bedroom blinds. "Down there's the barn and Travis's rig. See? I keep my town car in the barn so's it won't get dusty." She smiled. "Not that that helps a whole lot around here."

"Where's Travis? I don't see him."

"Maybe out behind. Depends on where those fool dogs led him."

"You don't seem very worried."

"My nephew can take care of himself. It's you I'm concerned about." She lowered her voice in spite of the fact they were alone in the house. "Are you just embarrassed to speak of it or have you really got amnesia?"

"I can't remember much," Emma admitted. "Some things are crystal clear, like knowing Travis by sight when I saw him in town. If I had amnesia, I wouldn't have known that, would I?"

"Beats me. I've got a nurse-practitioner friend who might be able to say. How about if I call her?"

"Maybe later. I'd like to clean up and rest first, if you don't mind."

"'Course. Where's my manners? I've got a brand-new jogging suit that should fit you. My sister sent it to me last Christmas," Cleo said, taking a clean towel out of a linen closet and handing it to Emma. "I've never worn the outfit and probably never will. It's just not my style."

She pointed. "Make yourself at home in this bathroom. Take as long as you need. I'll leave the clean clothes on the bed right outside this other door and you'll have all the privacy you want."

"I don't know how to thank you."

"All you need to think about now is taking care of yourself, honey. Don't worry about later. If my nephew gets too nosy, I'll put him in his place."

"I wish I…"

Cleo laid a gentle hand on Emma's arm through the sleeve of the gray sweatshirt. "Hush. Leave your dirty clothes outside in the hall and I'll see that they're washed and dried in a jiffy."

Touched, Emma brushed her bangs off her forehead with a shaky hand. "Thank you."

"No thanks needed. Just doin' my Christian duty. I'm glad you're a believer, too. It'll help you get better."

Was she? Emma wondered. She supposed she wouldn't have thought to pray before if she didn't believe in God, but she couldn't recall having been in a church for a long, long time.

That probably didn't matter to Him, she reasoned, calling to mind scraps of scripture promising faithfulness toward confessed believers. She could even picture herself, at a very young age, standing before her peers and reciting the week's memory verses.

Emma was smiling slightly as she turned and looked at her reflection in the mirror over the sink.

Her jaw dropped. Who was that weary, bruised waif looking back at her? There were dark circles and puffy half-moons beneath her reddened eyes. Her skin was unnaturally pale—except where a bruise as big as a fist colored one cheek. And her hair!

"Cleo was right," Emma muttered, embarrassed and

averting her gaze. "I'm bound to feel better after I shower and put on clean clothes."

And then what? What was she going to say when she finally emerged and rejoined the little family that had taken her in? How could she explain anything when her thoughts were as jumbled as the letter tiles in a spelling game, as tempest-tossed as dry leaves in an Arkansas tornado?

Fear of the unknown coursed through her. Not remembering being hurt might have given her temporary respite but now it was detrimental. As long as the face of her abuser remained lost in the labyrinth of her mind she was in continuing danger.

He—she was certain it had been a man—could walk up to her and she wouldn't recognize him. Or would she? There was no way to tell unless the meeting actually took place, and given the damage he'd already inflicted upon her, being face-to-face was the last thing she wanted.

Perhaps her reaction would be as instinctive as it had been when she'd seen Travis again. In the case of her nameless nemesis, she hoped and prayed she'd be aware enough to either flee or defend herself.

That thought reminded her of her race through the forest and the coarse shouts she'd heard behind her right before the shooting started.

That event was crystal clear. So why was she having so much trouble with the hours and days immediately preceding it?

Time will tell, Emma insisted. *It had better.*

Travis whistled his dogs out of the woods adjoining his main pasture and back to heel. They were panting, wagging their tails and obviously pleased with themselves.

"Too bad you guys can't talk," he told them. "I'd sure like to know what you were chasing out there."

Patting his thigh to bring them along, he'd just turned

and started back toward the house when he heard the rumbling echo of a motor. It didn't sound like a tractor or an ATV, more like a pickup truck, perhaps one with a diesel engine.

He and the dogs all froze. They looked west so he did, too. It was difficult to see far into the forest, even this early in the spring before the oak, sycamore and hickory trees leafed out.

Travis squinted against the rays of the setting sun. Something glinted in the distance before rising dust obliterated it.

Okay, so there was a vehicle out there where it didn't belong. That might be nothing more than a hunter training a dog or one of the neighbors chasing a loose cow. Many of the outlying areas weren't fenced. Anybody could have wandered onto his property without realizing they were trespassing.

If it hadn't been for Emma's paranoia he would have dismissed the incident.

Because of her, however, he jogged back to the house, penned the dogs to keep them safe, fired up his ATV and returned to where he'd glimpsed the reflection.

Dismounting, he bent over to examine the rutted dirt track, hardly more than a wide path through the forest. There were fresh tracks, all right. Looked like the tires of a heavy pickup with dual wheels in the rear. They led to a narrowing of the spaces between the trees where they stopped and reversed, thereby obliterating any crisp imprints.

Travis followed the trail for a short distance on foot. Sunset was near. His ability to spot the truck or anything else would soon be gone. But somebody had been there, just as his dogs had indicated.

And whoever it was had not been a local or he would have known that the trail he was on was impassible in a full-size vehicle. Therefore, the interloper had to have been a stranger. Could he have been after Emma, as she'd feared?

Only one thing was certain. While Emma was under his personal protection, he was going to make sure nobody got another chance to hurt her the way she had been before.

He set his jaw. After he sorted out all the details involved in keeping Emma safe from outsiders, he was going to have to face the roots of his own motives. Considering the way he instinctively reacted every time he saw her, he was afraid his protective urges were not as innocent as he'd been telling himself they were.

Pondering that emotional uncertainty, Travis returned to the ATV, fired it up and revved the engine. Its loud, rattling roar echoed through the otherwise silent forest.

Astride, he dropped the small vehicle in gear and took off for home. Before he had gone fifteen feet he sensed an imbalance and stopped to get off and check.

One of the two rear tires had gone flat. "Terrific. Just what I needed—a long walk home."

He crouched, expecting to spot what he'd carelessly run over in his haste to get back to the house.

The nearby trail was clean. No sharp rocks, no broken stubs or branches, nothing.

Before Travis could straighten again he heard the pop of a small-caliber rifle, followed by the singing whine of a bullet.

He ducked. Heard the shot impact the ATV. The flat tire was no accident! And now somebody was trying to flatten *him!*

Staying low, he duck-walked into the brush, then turned and headed cross-country instead of sticking to the normal trails. In the fall it might be possible for a foolish hunter to make the mistake of shooting at another human being because of the thick cover, but not this early in the year.

Whoever had been taking potshots at him had meant to do harm.

If he could have been certain that he wasn't outnumbered and outgunned, he might have stood his ground.

In this instance, however, there was only one thing on his mind. Getting back to Emma. Before it was too late.

THREE

Emma dressed in the comfortable lavender outfit Cleo had loaned her, then went back to the upstairs window while towel drying her hair. Shadows had lengthened, giving the farmyard a more somber aura. There sat Travis's truck and the stock trailer, just as he'd left them.

She unlocked the window and raised the sash to let in fresh air, inhaling deeply and sighing. No matter what was wrong with her, this was the best place to be. She didn't know how she could be so certain of that, yet she was. Her heart insisted.

The sound of barking dogs reached her and she listened carefully. They didn't sound angry anymore. Their yelps were shrill, as if they were keyed up and frustrated.

By leaning slightly to the side, Emma was able to view the source of the noise. All three of the dogs Travis had taken with him were confined in a pen next to the barn and jumping at the wire gate, acting frantic to escape.

Her throat tightened. Her pulse sped. If the dogs were there, where was Travis? Did he pen them up every night or was this evening different? There was only one way to find out.

Donning her tennis shoes, Emma hurried down the stairs in search of Cleo. They met in the kitchen where the older woman had hold of the old dog's collar while it whined and scratched at the back door.

"What's going on?"

Cleo was clearly worried. "Don't know. Bo all of a sudden wants out."

"Why not let him go?"

"Because I don't know what became of Travis. I heard him come back with the other dogs while you were taking your shower but then he hopped on the ATV and left again." She kept trying to calm the antsy hound.

"I could see from upstairs that he'd put the others in a pen. Is that normal?"

"No. We let the young ones patrol at night to keep the wild critters away from the chickens and such."

"Then call the police," Emma said, trying to mute her burgeoning fear.

"But you said…"

"I know what I said," Emma replied. "But that was when I thought I'd gotten away clean. If you think Travis is in trouble you need to call the authorities."

"What kind of trouble?" Cleo demanded. "Who's chasing you, girl?"

"I don't know. Honest, I don't. But I sense enough to be afraid. Do you have another gun?"

"Lots of 'em. This is hunting country. Why?"

"Because you should go arm yourself. Now." She reached for the collar. "I'll hold on to Bo for you."

She was glad to see Cleo was taking her seriously. The sense of foreboding she'd had all along was building so rapidly it was making her light-headed.

Alone in the kitchen, she closed her eyes for a momentary prayer, quickly coming to the conclusion she must act. But how? What could she do that would be sensible as well as useful? In the movies, a heroine always plunged into danger without a thought, often ending up in a worse fix.

She wasn't that foolish. Still, if Travis was in trouble, she also knew she couldn't just stand there like a deer frozen in the headlights of an oncoming car and wait for the worst.

Cleo returned with a shotgun and a box of shells. As her gaze met Emma's she hesitated. "You used to be a good shot. Is that part of your memory gone, too, or do you still know how to handle one of these if you have to?"

"It's mostly the last few months and years that are missing." She held out her hand. "Give me the gun. I know what to do."

"Not sure that's a good idea," Cleo said with a cautious shake of her head. "Not till we know what's wrong with you. No offense, but you might not be the most levelheaded person to carry this, even if it is kinda heavy for me."

"You're right. And it has been a long time since I was on the high-school skeet-shooting team."

"Bo's leash is hanging over there by the door. You can handle him," Cleo said, filling her pockets with loose shotgun shells. "I'll tote this double-barrel, at least for a ways."

"Shouldn't we wait for the sheriff?"

"No way. They said it'd be about twenty minutes when I called."

"Which leaves another fifteen. You're right. That's too long," Emma agreed. She reached for the leash and snapped it on the dog's collar before picking up a heavy-duty spotlight.

"Take it slow when you open the door and let me go out with the dog, first," Emma warned. "Just in case."

What remained unsaid was the ominous thought that the first person to step through that door might be in terrible jeopardy.

Nevertheless, Emma gathered her courage and led the way. To her surprise and relief, they made it off the porch and through the yard unscathed.

Beyond lay a deeper darkness, the kind that could hide more than a mere threat. It could mask death. And they'd never see it coming.

Travis kept to the trees as much as possible even though that wasn't the fastest way back to the ranch house. Until the last lingering rays of the sun vanished behind the hills he didn't want to try cutting across pastures and make himself an easier target.

After the first two shots into the ATV, he hadn't heard any more firing. That might mean his enemies had given up, or it might mean they were hot on his trail and could draw another bead at any moment.

Noises carried well on the still, late-evening air and were composed mostly of night birds and distant barking. "Sounds like my dogs have riled up every other canine for miles around, not to mention a few coyotes," he murmured, pausing to rest and recheck his surroundings from the edge of the forest.

Every window of his house glowed, making him wish he'd cautioned the women to pull the curtains and stay where they couldn't be seen. Surely, Cleo would think of that. She was a savvy old gal who was used to using her head for something besides a place to put a hat.

As Travis moved from tree to tree at the fringes of the rolling pasture he saw more lights come on at his place. The entire yard was now illuminated. The only advantage to that was being able to see if any strangers approached.

He suddenly saw movement at the rear of the house and heard Bo's distinctive baying. The old dog had struck a trail. Which meant somebody had let him out. That was not a good sign.

Travis peered around the trunk of a massive oak and scanned the area by the barn. He could see plenty from there and none of it was to his liking.

Two slightly built shadows had opened a pasture gate and were passing through with Bo in the lead. If he had to guess, he'd say Emma and Cleo were using the dog to track someone, probably him. Of all the lamebrained…

He watched the figures reach the periphery of the better-lit grounds and pause. One of them flicked on a strong beam of light and directed it at the straining, baying hound.

Travis was beside himself. Not only were the women out of the house, where they had no protection, they were lit up like a beacon, a perfect target for whoever had shot at him before.

Waving his arms and shouting, he did the only thing he could. He broke cover and ran headlong across the pasture toward the two most important people in his life.

A rifle cracked.

Travis dived for cover.

The spotlight went out.

A woman screamed.

"Stay down!" Emma shouted, tugging on Cleo's arm to bring her closer to the ground.

"Did you see where that shot came from?"

"No. But I think I did see somebody fall. All I got was a glimpse. Did you see it, too?"

"Yes. Let the dog loose so we can tell which direction he goes without sticking our heads up."

"I think I hear sirens," Emma said. "Must be the sheriff. Finally."

"Who is sure gonna wonder what became of me after I called," Cleo added, sounding disgusted. "Think we can crawl all the way back?"

"I doubt we'll have to. I imagine the lights and sirens will scare off whoever's out there." She raised up slightly, pushed the handheld light as far away from them as she could reach, then turned it on again before scrambling back to Cleo.

Nothing happened. Nobody shot. Bo had disappeared and had quit baying.

A patrol car stopped in the farmyard. Officers got out, drew their guns and headed for the gaping kitchen door.

Emma took Cleo's elbow to help her up. "I think we're safe now. You keep the shotgun and head straight for the police car. I'll be right behind you."

Since the pasture was used for grazing it didn't have to be perfectly flat, meaning that Cleo and Emma both did their share of stumbling as they tried to hurry.

As Cleo reached the metal gate, Emma paused. Her companion was safe. Trouble was, they still didn't know what had become of Travis.

A shiver skittered up her spine. Emma froze. Turned on her heel. Stared into the dimness.

Could the falling figure have been Travis? She supposed so. Either him or whoever had shot at them, and given the opposing directions, she judged the rifle to have been farther away and to the left.

Sounds of muffled steps in the dry stubble of grass reached her. Someone was coming her way. Fast.

Shadows moved. Bent over the light Emma had abandoned in the field. It swung to briefly shine on her, then was turned up to illuminate a face.

"Travis!"

"Don't shoot at me again, okay?"

Emma was adamant. "We never shot at anything. Besides, Cleo brought a shotgun. What we heard was a rifle, or have you forgotten what one sounds like?"

He was beside her quickly. "I haven't forgotten a thing. But apparently you have. What happened to being scared? I thought you were petrified that some bad guy would catch up to you."

"I was. I still am." She shook him off when he tried to cup her elbow.

"Then what are you doing out of the house?"

"We were worried about you. Bo was acting up so we decided to come look for you while we waited for the sheriff."

"Not the smartest thing either of you has ever done."

"You don't hear me arguing, do you?"

"When we get to the gate, make a run for the house. I'll cover you."

"Against who? We never saw a thing, did you?"

"Just because you don't see a copperhead doesn't mean he's not fixing to bite you," Travis said flatly.

Emma could tell he was struggling to control his temper and she didn't blame him. She and Cleo had both let their emotions get the better of their common sense and they were fortunate nothing worse had happened.

Doing as she'd been told, she darted through the gate and raced for the back porch. Just as she reached the steps, Bo galloped past her and through the open door.

Emma sensed rather than saw Travis until he slammed the door behind them. Her soul-deep relief was so strong, so genuine, she almost turned and hugged him.

Judging by his poignant expression when her eyes met his, he wouldn't have pushed her away if she had given in and stepped into his arms.

Sheriff Harlan Allgood had remained behind while his deputy returned to the station, promising to check the woods and help retrieve the disabled ATV in daylight.

Cleo had made a fresh pot of coffee and everyone was gathered around the kitchen table.

Travis had barely taken his eyes off Emma since they'd returned to the house. He was still trying to decide if she'd been acting foolishly because she cared about him or because her mind was too scrambled to think logically. Or both.

"I get little flashes of things," Emma said in reply to the sheriff's questioning. "It's like I'm starting to remember and then my brain shuts down."

"What do you think you're seeing? Any clues may help, even if you can't make sense of them yet."

Travis grasped his coffee mug tightly as he watched Emma's emotional struggles.

She closed her eyes, then said, "I remember running away. I was terrified and somebody was chasing me."

"Where was this?" Harlan asked, speaking softly.

"I don't know. It was dark out when I finally got a door open and escaped." Her brow knit before her eyes popped open. "I ran past some parked trucks! Pickups. Then I hit the woods."

Her fingertips touched her cheeks. "There were lots of brambles—like sticker vines—hanging from the trees. They were so thick it was hard to get through them at all."

"Meaning you were probably still in the South," Cleo ventured.

"Yes!" Emma sounded encouraged. "And it only took me a day or so to hitchhike home, so it couldn't have been far." She glanced over at Travis. "Did I say anything about that when you picked me up?"

"No. I had to work to even see your face at first," he replied, taking care to try to keep his voice neutral. "All you wanted was to go home, so I brought you here."

With a deep sigh, Emma nodded. "That's right. You reminded me that my father had passed on and Mom had moved away. I sort of knew that. I seem to recall that she went to California to live with her sister."

Harlan agreed. "That's right. Do you want me to see if I can get ahold of her for you?"

Travis wasn't surprised to see Emma shake her head.

"No," she said. "Not yet. Not until I know what's really going on and who has been chasing me. I mean, why me? What can I have done that would make anybody want to lock me up or hurt me?" Her hand drifted to her bruised cheek.

There were unshed tears in her eyes as she looked to Travis, then Cleo, before focusing on the portly lawman. "I have made up my mind about one thing, though. I'm not staying here. I've brought enough trouble to these folks and as long as I'm around, it won't stop."

Cleo started to reach for Emma's hand. Travis beat her to it. "Don't be silly. Where else can you go?"

"I don't know. But I'm not staying on with you. Look what's happened already."

The sheriff cleared his throat. "To be fair, you don't really know the incident in the woods had anything to do with you, Miss Emma. Could have been poachers or just some rowdies."

Travis disagreed but chose to keep that opinion to himself. If Emma left the ranch, there would be no way he could continue to look after her. And, if her vague memories ever fully returned, he figured she'd need a friend. Someone like him, who truly cared for her. Plus, Cleo was a stabilizing influence and nearly as capable of defending her as he was, providing she didn't go on any more quests after dark.

The sheriff cleared his throat and got to his feet. "Well, if there's nothing else, I'll be going. Thanks for the coffee, Miz Cleo. I'll see you tomorrow, Travis. You'll need to show me where you left your ATV so we can have a look at it."

Cleo arose to walk Harlan to the door while Travis remained with Emma, still grasping her hand, tightly yet gently, and rubbing the back of it with his thumb.

"How bad is it?" he asked in a near whisper. "When you have these flashes of memory, how bad is it?"

Emma closed her eyes. A single tear slid down her cheek. "I see colors, dark colors, and red, like blood. Bits of faces, too, peering at me through slatted blinds." She took a shuddering breath. "I want to look away but I can't. Sometimes there's cursing, and creepy laughter, as if the person is enjoying torturing me."

"I'm so sorry," Travis said gently.

Emma's eyes suddenly popped open. She gasped, covering her mouth with her free hand.

Travis leaned closer. "What is it? What else did you just remember?"

"It can't be." Emma's breathing was shallow and rapid, as though she'd just run a marathon.

"What? Tell me."

More tears spilled out and wet her bruised cheek. "A child. I see a child. A little blonde girl."

Travis gave in and put his arms around her as she began to weep in earnest. "Easy, honey. Maybe it's just your imagination."

"No." Emma was adamant. "I—I saw her. And I felt her. She was holding my hand. She trusted me. And for some reason I left her." Emma turned her tearstained face up to Travis and asked, "How could I *do* such a thing?"

He had no answer for her. Or for himself.

FOUR

Emma had never been fond of the night, but darkness had seldom frightened her as much as it now did.

She had let Cleo escort her upstairs and loan her a flannel nightgown while Travis stayed behind to double-check the locks on the doors and windows.

His footfalls on the stairs were a welcome sound, particularly after she opened her door a crack and peeked out to watch him pass before shutting it tightly. There was no lock on her door; nor would she have used it if there had been. It was enough to know she wasn't alone in the house.

What was almost as frightening as reality was the notion of the nightmares that sleep might bring. Emma knew she couldn't lie awake all night, yet the moment she closed her eyes she feared the glimpses of evil would return.

Finally, unable to stay alert any longer, she pulled the covers up under her chin, sighed and closed her eyes.

Soon, it began.

The room of her dreams was dark and dank. The cot on which she lay was lumpy, her lone blanket scratchy and frayed. She tried to move her left arm and found it bound by something cold and metallic that was cutting into her wrist.

Her eyes popped open. Someone was coming! A key

clicked in the lock and the metal door swung open with a squeal of its rusty hinges.

A huge shape loomed. Approached.

Emma cringed, fisting the blanket and peering into the darkness to try to see details of the man's shadowed face. The brightness behind him prevented it. "What do you want?"

"You know what I want. The sooner you tell me where my useless wife stashed the goods, the sooner you'll be free to go."

Emma's mouth was so dry she could barely speak. "I don't know what you're talking about."

"Ha!" His laugh was cruel and cynical. "She only had one close friend and you were it. You must know."

"I don't. Please, let me go. I won't tell anybody what you've done. I promise I won't."

"Like you promised my wife you'd keep her secret?"

"Yes. I mean, no. I don't have any secrets to keep."

Hovering over the cot, he leaned closer. Emma could smell alcohol on his breath, sense an anger so great it was smothering.

He drew back his arm.

She cringed, knowing what was coming.

The shadowy figure swung his open hand and Emma heard it connect with her cheek, felt the sting of the blow.

She managed to inhale past the lump in her throat and screamed.

Travis lay atop the comforter, still dressed except for his boots, in case he needed to take quick action again. Harlan might have been right about the shots that had disabled the ATV, but it was just as easy to imagine that Emma's foes had found her, particularly since she'd returned to her roots. Anybody who knew where she'd come from would be able to track her.

The only sounds were familiar: the house settling, an occasional call of a whip-poor-will outside and the yips from a restless pack of coyotes somewhere in the woods. If Travis's mind had not been so busy trying to figure out what was going on regarding his houseguest, he would already have drifted off to sleep.

His eyelids were getting heavy when the silence was suddenly broken by a high-pitched screech.

He was on his feet before he even realized he was moving. *Emma!*

Just as he reached for the doorknob of her room it was jerked away.

Wild-eyed, hands pressed over her mouth, she barreled headlong into his chest.

Travis barely managed to keep his balance. "Easy, Emma, I've got you," he said, holding her gently in spite of her pummeling fists.

Thankfully, the strength of her attack was waning.

"Breathe, honey, breathe," he urged. "Come on, Emma, take a deep breath. You're safe."

To his relief, the panic-filled haze seemed to clear. She blinked. Focused. Drew in air with a shudder.

"Travis."

His name was hardly more than a whisper, but it was enough to prove to him that she was fully awake and aware.

"That's right, it's Travis. You're in my house and you're safe. I promise."

"I thought…"

"What, Emma? What did you think? Tell me. It might help us find out what happened to you."

She was still gulping air. "I—I was dreaming. It was awful."

"What can you remember?"

"A man. Big. He—he was asking me something. I couldn't remember then, either, so he hit me."

"What else? Did the dream tell you where you were?"

She shook her head. "No. Only in a room somewhere. And a cot. I was lying on a cot." Easing away from Travis, she held out one arm and stared at her reddened wrist. "It wasn't a rope that made this mark, it was handcuffs. I was fastened to the bedpost with a chain."

Although her look of terror was gone it had been replaced with a sense of absolute truth that cut Travis to the quick. Someone had kept Emma prisoner all right. But who? Why? And how in the world had she managed to escape?

"How did you get away?"

Slowly, pensively, she shook her head. "I don't know."

"Did you have help? Was there someone else there with you? Maybe that child you thought you recalled?"

He could see her struggling to remember. It was in her eyes, in her expression, in the way she leaned a little away from him so she could meet his somber gaze.

"I don't know," Emma finally said. "In this nightmare I was all alone—except for the man who hit me." Her hand raised to cup her cheek. "Right there, just the way it looks."

They were joined by Cleo, belting a robe and padding barefoot down the hallway. "Land sakes. What's going on?"

"Emma had a nightmare," Travis explained. "I heard her screaming and thought she was being attacked again."

The older woman put her arms around both Emma and Travis. "Praise the Lord it wasn't for real."

"She remembered a few things because of it," Travis added. "It wasn't a pleasant experience but it might help her recover in the long run."

Blinking, Emma looked from one to the other, her eyes misty. "I'm afraid to go to sleep for fear more of it will come back to me, yet I want to know. Does that sound as crazy to you as it does to me?"

"Not crazy at all," Cleo said calmly. "Since we're all wide-awake, how about going downstairs for a cup of hot chocolate? That always helps me relax."

Emma was quick to agree so Travis did, too. Given a choice, he would gladly have stood in that hallway for hours, comforting Emma. There was nothing wrong with *his* memory. He remembered exactly how she had felt in his arms. And how deeply he'd been hurt when her letters to him had stopped so abruptly.

Every muscle in his body tensed. Could that have been when she first got into trouble? Maybe, if he'd gone to look for her then…

You can't change the past, he told himself. *Even if you could, there's no guarantee you'd have been able to locate Emma, particularly if she didn't want to be found.*

That was how it had seemed to everyone, he recalled. At first, her letters had been upbeat and joyful, even when she was relating failed auditions. Then, their tone had changed and they had finally stopped coming. He'd thought surely she'd return for her father's funeral two years ago, but she hadn't even done that.

Now, for the first time since, Travis wondered if she'd already been a prisoner then. The thought was so disquieting it caused him physical pain.

The mug's warmth as her hands clasped it was nearly as comforting as the hot beverage. Emma had accepted the long coat Cleo had given her in lieu of a proper robe and was seated at the kitchen table with the others.

"I'm glad you asked me questions as soon as I woke up," Emma said. "I'm already starting to forget the details of my nightmare."

Travis smiled slightly and began to enumerate. "So far, we know you were locked up and escaped. The place could have been anywhere. Do you think it was near Nashville? That's where your last letters came from."

"How long ago was that?"

"Several years. You were supposed to be coming back to Serenity for your father's funeral but you never showed. Your mom was devastated when she didn't hear from you. She tried to get the police to look for you but nobody would believe there was anything wrong."

"Why not?"

He cleared his throat and took a slow sip, clearly buying time. "You'd been singing with a band that often got into trouble."

"Trouble?" Emma frowned. "What kind of trouble?"

"Let's just say their reputation was not for reliability. Or honesty."

"I can't imagine I'd put up with that. I always felt my music was very important. That's why…" Blushing, she averted her gaze.

"I know. You made that quite clear when you refused to stay here and marry me."

Her lips parted, trembling. "I really did that?"

"Yes."

"Enough of all this," Cleo interjected. "Let's get back to the dream. What else can you tell us?"

"Only that it could just as easily have been a product of my imagination," Emma said sadly. "That's exactly what it feels like now."

"Doesn't mean there can't be a ring of truth to it," the older woman insisted. "Your injuries prove you were held prisoner and chained up. Think about the rest of the room. What did it look like? Smell like? What could you hear in the background when it was quiet?"

Emma pursed her lips. "There was a rotten smell, like garbage. And a tiny bathroom. Sometimes I thought I heard muffled voices but I could never understand what they were saying."

"How about music?"

Her eyes widened. "Yes! Guitar, with an amped-up bass that sometimes rumbled through the floor."

"Now we're getting somewhere," Travis said. "What else?"

Emma's shoulders slumped and she sighed. "That's it. That's all. I'm sorry."

Patting her hand, Cleo was reassuring. "You've come a long way since you got here. I have a nurse-practitioner friend who might be able to help, too."

"I don't want to go anywhere. Not until I'm sure nobody is out to get me."

"Do you mind if I invite her over for supper? Come to think of it, you may have gone to school with her. Remember Samantha Rochard?"

"Vaguely. I think she was a couple years ahead of me."

"Probably. She married John Waltham."

"That name rings a bell, too. What does he do?"

"He's with the police," Cleo said, arching a brow. "If there's a crime involved, like we suspect, and we can convince Samantha of it, she can go to work on John for us and maybe get some action."

Although she nodded in agreement, Emma kept thinking of her tenuous past and the possibility that she had been keeping company with criminals. In her heart she felt innocent, yet that didn't mean she hadn't been in as much trouble as her current predicament indicated. Kidnappers didn't go around chaining up harmless people. She must have done something to have brought this on herself. But what?

A shadowy image danced at the fringes of her consciousness, looming then retreating like a phantom.

She squeezed her eyes tightly closed and concentrated.

The face began to solidify, to leer at her with stained, crooked teeth and piercing blue eyes. She knew that face! It had been a part of her life even before the abduction.

And with that picture of the man came another glimpse of the little blonde girl. Only this time it was he who was holding her hand.

A light touch jolted Emma. Both Travis and his aunt were staring at her, asking questions with their concerned expressions.

"I just saw more," Emma whispered. "The man who hit me had blue eyes and bad teeth."

"That's wonderful," Travis told her.

She shook her head adamantly. "No. It's worse. The little girl? The one I told you I sort of remembered?"

Travis nodded.

"I think I know why I left without her," Emma said. "She apparently belongs to that horrible man who locked me up."

Reaching out to tightly grasp Travis's hand, she added, "We have to find her and get her away from him somehow. We *have* to."

It was almost dawn before Travis was able to get back to sleep, and even then his restlessness prevented adequate rest.

Sometime after they had all retired again it had occurred to him to do a computer search for Emma and the band she had been with before dropping out of sight. Given that she would be a definite asset during that kind of research, he had opted to wait until the following morning.

He was already seated at the kitchen table with his laptop open and coffee brewed when the women joined him.

Cleo donned an apron and went to work at the stove, as usual, while Emma poured herself a cup of hot coffee, carried it to the table and paused behind him. "What're you doing? Email?"

Travis shook his head. "No. I've been waiting for you to get up so I could show you a few things I found already." He pulled up some sites he'd saved. "Does any of this promo look familiar?"

"No. I don't think so."

As she leaned closer she rested one hand lightly on his shoulder, sending a shiver zinging from his toes to the top of his head.

Travis ignored the pleasant sensation to ask, "How about this one? The band's name is similar to the one you used to sing with."

She was shaking her head. "No. Sorry."

It wasn't until the fifth photo spread that he heard Emma's sharp intake of breath and felt her hand grip his shoulder more tightly as she set her coffee cup aside.

"Wait. Go back. That guitar player on the left looks familiar."

"I thought he might," Travis said. "When you described your captor last night I immediately thought of Blake."

"Who?"

"Blake Browning." Travis pointed at the screen. "He's the guy you chose over me and went to Nashville with."

"I did?" Her brow was knit, her eyes narrowing as she stared. "I can't believe it. Him? Over you?"

Apparently realizing how her comments could be misconstrued, Emma immediately straightened and backed away from Travis, giving him room to turn and look up at her.

"It was probably the chance to become a star that swayed you. I can see that now. But at the time it seemed awfully personal."

"I can understand how it might," she replied somberly. "There's a lot I don't recall, but I'm positive I was never romantically involved with that man. Just looking at his photo makes my skin crawl."

"I guess that's a good sign," Travis said. "I tried to trace him and the Browning Brothers band and came up empty. We'll probably have to let Harlan take it from here."

The lack of enthusiasm showing on Emma's still-bruised face told him she didn't consider his suggestion to be a good one.

"You and I can do more research later if you want," Travis promised. "Right now, I need to have breakfast and get ready to take the sheriff and his deputies to where I left the four-wheeler. They're supposed to be here at eight."

"I'm going with you," Emma declared.

Travis had not expected that. Therefore, his retort was less than diplomatic. "No, you're not. You're staying in this house with Cleo."

Judging by the way Emma's hands were fisted on her hips, he realized she had not taken kindly to his forceful-ness. All she said was, "Oh?"

He pushed away from the table, stood and closed the laptop before reaching for her hand. "I didn't mean that the way it sounded. Think, Emma. Whoever was out there last night may still be hanging around. If it was Blake, he'd know you and I used to be close. This is one of the first places he'd look for you."

"There's also nobody who knows what he looks like as well as I do."

"I thought you didn't remember."

She shook her head and pressed her lips into a thin line as if sorting her thoughts before speaking. "I don't remem-ber many details of being kept prisoner, but I do know what it feels like to look into that man's eyes."

"Do the two go together?" Travis asked.

Emma blinked rapidly. "I'm not sure. The person I see when glimpses of a face come to me seems darker, more menacing. But it could just be shadows I'm remembering. Nothing is clear."

"Okay. I'll buy that. Aunt Cleo's nurse friend is coming over this evening and maybe she can help us all understand what's got your thoughts so scrambled." He gave Emma's hand a gentle squeeze. "In the meantime, will you please stay out of sight? For Cleo's sake, if not for mine?"

"Well, when you put it that way…"

Before she could change her mind he smiled, took his half-empty coffee mug to the sink and headed for the back door.

Keeping that headstrong young woman safe was far more important than taking time to eat a proper breakfast. He'd grab a bite later, after he'd shown Harlan the damaged ATV and hauled it back to the barn.

As a last-minute act he once again grabbed the pistol off the top of the kitchen cabinet and securely clipped its holster to his belt before pulling on a denim jacket.

Travis was far from certain that his enemies had abandoned their attempts to do harm. Even if they didn't happen to be lurking in the woods anymore, they were around. He felt it all the way to the marrow of his bones.

And he didn't intend to give them any advantages if he could help it.

One final glance at Emma was all he allowed himself. The sight of her standing there, arms folded and looking so forlorn, was nearly enough to make him backtrack and give her a parting hug.

That would be a really stupid move, he decided in seconds. The best way to keep his wits about him and succeed in protecting her was to remain aloof and encourage her to do the same.

He huffed. He was already so emotionally involved with Emma Landers he could barely see straight. And that could prove fatal. To both of them.

FIVE

The warmth and homey aromas of the farm kitchen wrapped around Emma like a security blanket. She forced a smile for Cleo's sake and tried to stop worrying about Travis. "Whatever you're fixing smells wonderful."

"That'd be the fresh corn bread," the older woman said. "Don't fret about my nephew. He can take care of himself.

"I know." Emma made a face. "I just feel so responsible for all this. I wish he'd at least let me help him bring the ATV back."

"Leave that to the men. They'll never admit we can handle things as well as they do." She chuckled. "I always used to wait till my Jim was real busy, then fix the things around the house that he didn't have time for. I know he must have noticed but he never said a word about it."

"Travis told me he inherited this ranch. That seems kind of odd. Why didn't co-ownership pass to you?"

"Country ways, mostly," Cleo told her. "Around here, they're more concerned with blood ties to the land than with marriage ones. Jim left me plenty of money to buy myself a house in town but I didn't want to move. And since Travis needed me, I stayed put."

"You weren't upset? I mean, your husband cut you out."

"I'd known all about his plans for years," Cleo said.

"Since there are no community property laws in Arkansas, I just accepted it as inevitable and didn't argue."

"It seems so old-fashioned."

"That doesn't make it wrong," Cleo countered. "It's like Travis tellin' you to stay in the house. I could see it rankled, but that's no proof he was wrong."

Emma had to laugh. "All right. I get the idea. But if he keeps ordering me around I'm liable to argue."

Grinning, the older woman gave her a conspiratorial wink. "I can hardly wait to hear it."

Sheriff Harlan Allgood drove out to the site of the shooting in his patrol car after Travis and a deputy named Adelaide Crowe crossed the pasture in Travis's farm truck and radioed GPS coordinates.

The damaged ATV was just as he'd left it, complete with flat tire and a hole through one fender.

"Looks like this was done with a .22," Harlan observed. "Probably won't be much left of the slug to retrieve and even if we could, ballistics won't help unless we have a weapon to match it to."

Travis shrugged, his hands in his jacket pockets. "I know. I suppose I could have just towed the thing home without bothering you, but I was concerned that this might have something to do with Emma."

"She still claimin' amnesia?"

"In a manner of speaking," Travis replied. "There are times when she seems to remember bits and pieces, then other times when she hardly knows her own name." He pulled a face. "That's an exaggeration. She does know that. And she seems to know me. It's the past few years that only come to her in fits and starts."

Straightening from where she'd been examining the damaged vehicle, Adelaide looked to her boss. "Kind of reminds me of what Thad Pearson went through with PTSD.

Remember? Just because a person hasn't actually fought in a war doesn't mean they can't be traumatized."

"Cleo and I thought of that," Travis said. "Samantha Rochard-Waltham is coming to the house tonight to give Emma a good looking-over. Maybe she can at least put a name to the problem so we don't have to keep wondering."

The female deputy was scanning the surrounding forest. "How many times did you say you were shot at?"

"Twice. Once in the tire and once in the rear fender. Why?"

Instead of answering immediately, Adelaide took out a pocket knife and began probing the bark of a nearby hickory sapling. She turned in moments to display her find.

Travis didn't have to be told what she'd found. The revving noise of his engine had apparently masked more shots than he'd registered. And the bullet she had just dug out of the tree must have barely missed him!

A shiver raced up his spine and prickled the hair on the back of his neck. His intent stare traced the path of the shot from the depths of the distant woods to the tree. Why that attempt had not taken him down was a wonder. Or, as Cleo would say, his guardian angel now had a lot more gray hair.

"I never heard that one coming," he told the sheriff. "Guess I must have leaned forward at just the right time."

"No guess about it," Harlan said, frowning and turning away to scan the distant terrain. "Deputy Crowe, you go scout over there, just in case somebody dropped another clue. In the meantime, Travis and I are gonna have us a little talk."

When the sheriff looked back at Travis his scowl had deepened. "You're protectin' Emma, aren't you?"

"No." He held up a hand. "I swear I'm not holding anything back. She's so befuddled it's not funny. Under the circumstances, I'm surprised she made it back to Serenity."

"She remembered that much?"

"Up to a point. It seems as though she's aware of her childhood and some of her teen years. It's after she left town, where she went, and who she was with, that's foggy."

"Or, so she claims."

"I believe her," Travis said, hoping Harlan would continue to give Emma the benefit of the doubt for a little longer. "She comes up with a detail here and there but it's hard to track her thoughts. I'm pretty sure she'll eventually be able to put the whole story together to suit everybody, herself included."

What Travis chose to keep to himself for the present was Emma's impression that an unnamed child might be in jeopardy. That story was mixed up and kept changing too much. Until Emma settled on an indisputable fact he figured it was best to say nothing rather than send the law off on a tangent. If her tales of an endangered child took shape and proved true, then he'd gladly act.

"All right," the portly sheriff said. "I'll help you push that crippled machine to your truck before I try to turn my rig around. You couldn't have picked a nastier place to have your ambush."

"Believe me, Harlan, I didn't pick it." Travis took the ATV out of gear and started to maneuver it as best he could. It wasn't easy, particularly with a flat tire. "I've been thinking about the tire tracks I spotted last night. Local boys wouldn't be likely to pull a big rig out here. The trail's too narrow. Besides, it was getting dark. They'd be crazy to get themselves into a tight spot like this."

"Crazy is right," the sheriff replied. "Anybody who'd take potshots at a stranger on his own land has to be nuts."

"Maybe they knew me."

That remark brought instant attention. "You saw the shooter?"

"No." Travis shook his head. "But while you're investigating, you might want to see where Blake Browning is hanging out these days."

"Why him? I haven't laid eyes on him or his brother, Ben, for ages."

"None of us have. It's just that I remembered it was Blake's band that Emma joined when she left for Nashville."

"You think he might be lookin' for her? Why?"

"I don't know. He may not be. All I'm sure about is that she recognized a photo of him I found on the internet and it upset her. A lot."

"Could be she just quit his group and he got somebody else. I reckon there's plenty of hopeful singers in a place like Nashville."

"There's only one that I care about," Travis said flatly. "Will you check for me? Please?"

The sheriff shrugged as they positioned the small, single-person vehicle at the bottom of a pair of ramps and hooked a cable to its front tow hook. "Okay. I'll see what I can find out. But don't hold your breath. I remember Mrs. Landers asking me to do the same thing a couple of years ago after her husband died. It was like everybody in that whole Browning Brothers band had dropped clean off the face of the earth after one of their members copped a plea and went to prison."

"You'll still try again?"

They began to winch the heavy ATV aboard the pickup. "I'll try," Harlan promised. His gaze wandered to the tree where his deputy had extracted the small bullet. "And in the meantime, it might be good if you kept your head down and minded your own business."

"Yeah," Travis said with a grimace. "I think that's a very good idea." *Too bad it wasn't going to be possible.*

* * *

"Is there anything I can do to help you?" Emma asked Cleo.

"Just keep me company while I brown this roast for supper and get it in the oven. Later, you and I can set the dining-room table for company."

"All right. I wonder what's taking Travis so long?"

"I heard him drive in a while back. He's probably out in the barn tinkering with the ATV."

The house phone rang.

Smiling, Cleo held up hands dusty with flour and asked, "Can you get that for me?"

"Sure." Without hesitation, Emma reached for the receiver of the instrument hanging on the wall. It struck her as odd to see such an old-fashioned phone when most people used cells.

"Wright Ranch," was all she said.

The muffled laugh on the other end of the line caused her to scowl. "Hello? Hello? I'm sorry, I can't hear you."

"You heard plenty last night, didn't you, Emma," the voice drawled.

Anger rose in her. "Who is this? What do you want with me?"

"You already know."

"No!" She was shouting into the receiver. "I don't know. I can't remember a thing. Leave me alone!"

"Humph. That ain't gonna happen. You know it and I know it, so stop pretending or you and your boyfriend will both be sorry." He guffawed eerily. "And the old lady, too. Maybe I'll start with her. That should jog your memory."

By this time Cleo was beside Emma, their ears pressed close so both could listen. Instead of butting into the conversation, Cleo used one floury finger on the disconnect lever to break the connection.

"No sense giving scum like that the courtesy of listening. The next time that phone rings, you let me or Travis answer."

"It will ring again, won't it?" Emma's knees were wobbly, her vision blurred by unshed tears. "Even if I left this very minute, that person might still bother you." *And maybe really hurt you,* she added to herself.

The instinct to run and not look back was strong. The realization that doing so in the past had not helped kept her from fleeing again.

All right, she decided, squaring her shoulders and taking a settling breath in spite of her quaking nerves. *If I can't protect the people I care about by leaving, I'll do it by standing my ground and facing my enemies.*

Beyond that vow lay the awareness that she needed to call upon God, as well. She might not recall worshipping recently but she knew her heavenly Father was still there, still listening, still willing to forgive, even if she couldn't name her sins.

Asking His forgiveness wasn't hard.

Believing it had been granted, however, was a totally different story.

"You should go tell Travis what just happened," Cleo suggested, breaking into her thoughts. "We need to all be on the same page so we're not caught unawares."

"I agree." Emma grabbed the freshly washed gray sweatshirt and slipped it on over the jogging-suit jacket. "I'll run out to the barn and talk to him."

"I'll watch till you get there in case I have to come after you with my shotgun."

"I wish I felt it was safe for me to be armed, but until I know more about why I'm so confused, I suspect it will be best for me to stay away from firearms."

"Just the fact you're sayin' that makes me trust your judgment more," Cleo said. "After you've talked to Samantha tonight, for starters, we'll consider making changes."

Emma paused at the door, her hand on the knob. "Do you honestly think she can help me?"

"God willing," Cleo said tenderly, smiling. "Trust Him the way you used to when you were a little girl, honey. He'll be there for you. I know He will."

Emma truly wanted to believe that. She simply wasn't positive. Not yet.

Knowing that his aunt and Emma were safe within the house, Travis made use of his opportunity to tinker with the ATV and do some serious thinking in private. When Emma was around he found it impossible to ignore her, particularly since she was so desperately in need of his aid.

Would she have come back to me if she'd had any other choice? he asked himself. Perhaps. Perhaps not. It was a moot point since she was there and he was already up to his neck in her problems.

Startled by a shadow crossing in front of the open doorway and his ranch dogs getting to their feet, Travis fisted a wrench and crouched defensively behind the ATV.

Emma appeared. She was smiling, hands raised, palms out, as the dogs crowded around her with wagging tails. "Whoa. Take it easy, Travis. It's just me."

Just her? He almost laughed out loud. There was nothing simple or trivial about Emma. If there had been, maybe his heart would quit jumping every time he saw her.

"What's up?" He wiped his hands on a rag as nonchalantly as he could and laid it aside with the wrench while she busied herself paying special attention to each friendly hound.

Emma finally met his gaze. "Cleo and I thought… I mean, we decided…"

"I've got that much," Travis said with a lazy smile. "You women have come to some kind of conclusion that involves me. So, spill it."

Her smile waned and she nodded soberly. "Somebody just called the house. Cleo was busy cooking so I answered."

Judging by the way the healthy color had drained from Emma's cheeks, the caller had not been friendly. Travis circled the half-dismantled vehicle and touched her sleeve. "Who was it?"

"I don't know. Cleo came over and we both listened a bit before she hung up for me. It was a man making threats. Against me and both of you, too."

"What exactly did he say?"

Emma pressed her fingertips to her temples. "He seemed to think I was keeping a secret of some kind. I told him I couldn't remember but he didn't believe me."

"I kept meaning to put caller ID on my phones. Never got around to it. I think it's time I did that." He had cupped her elbow and was urging her toward the house as he spoke, pausing only long enough to scan the quiet yard and make sure his dogs were not showing signs of sensing trespassers.

"What am I going to do?" Emma had to nearly run to keep up with his long strides.

"We're going to report this to Harlan for starters," Travis said. "Whoever it is can't get away with harassing you."

"Do you think it's Blake?"

"I don't know. Was the voice familiar?"

Emma was shaking her head. "I don't think so. It was sort of muffled and deep. Even so, I think I'd have recognized some similarities if it had been him."

"That's what I was afraid of," Travis said, hustling her up the back steps and into the kitchen. "Even if he is involved, I don't think he's acting alone."

"Which means we're back to square one."

"Not exactly."

Travis drew the blinds over the kitchen window above

the sink and locked the back door before picking up the telephone, dialing and asking to speak with the sheriff.

Cleo and Emma concentrated on his every word, supplying little details, as needed, when he relayed Harlan's questions.

"No. There was no more shooting," Travis assured him. "Not this time. But he scared the daylights out of the women with his phone threats."

"I wouldn't go that far," Cleo interjected, sounding miffed.

Travis ignored her to continue his main conversation. "That's right. They had the number for the house. No, not my cell. Why? Okay." He nodded sagely. "I understand. I'll keep my head down."

As he ended the call he became aware of added scrutiny. Meeting his aunt's gaze boldly, he tried to will her to let the subject drop. She didn't.

"Okay. Why should Harlan tell you to keep your head down? I thought the yahoos in the woods were just shooting at your tires."

"There may have been a few more shots that I wasn't aware of at the time," Travis said, shrugging off her concern. "It's not important. There was no harm done."

A sidelong glance at Emma told him that she was taking his confession even harder than Cleo was. Her skin was ashen, her blue eyes wide.

"All right. This is how it is," Travis explained. "Whoever is chasing Emma has figured out where she's staying and is apparently determined to get her to reveal some secret she actually can't remember." He concentrated on her. "Is that right?"

Emma nodded. She had laced her slim fingers together so tightly they were turning white.

"And you truly don't have a clue why he's after you?"

"No! I've told you over and over. *I do not know.*"

"Okay, let's suppose that's true and…"

Emma shouted, "It *is* true."

"Bad choice of words," he countered, still not totally convinced she wasn't withholding something, even if she didn't realize she was doing it. "The sheriff is going to send someone out to put a device on this line that will record all incoming calls and their origins. In the meantime, he suggests we use cell phones, instead. Those numbers should be harder to come by."

Emma sank into a kitchen chair. "I just want it all to be over."

Cleo joined her and slipped an arm around her shoulders. "Tell you what. How about I get the rest of the dinner preparations finished and we run into town to get you some decent clothes. You'll feel better once you have some nice things of your own to wear."

Travis was astonished. "I don't believe you two. Don't you understand what's going on? None of us should even stick our heads outside unless we absolutely have to—and you're talking about going *shopping*."

"In a busy store in a crowd," Cleo said. "We'll run over to Ash Flat to that big-box store." She smiled. "If you're so worried, you can drive us there."

"Well, you're sure not going alone," he said, gritting his teeth as he stared at his aunt.

"Then it's settled. Just give me another half hour and I'll be ready."

Travis looked to Emma. "You're going along with this crazy plan?"

She seemed to regain a more natural color as she straightened her spine, lifted her chin and faced him. "I've made up my mind that the only way to cope is to face my fears," Emma said. "Might as well start today."

It took all the self-control Travis could muster to hold his tongue—and his temper.

SIX

Emma didn't blame Travis for watching his rearview mirrors as though he expected more trouble. She did, too. Sort of.

Feeling strangely calm considering their situation, she sat wedged in the center of the farm truck's front seat while Cleo occupied the place by the window.

Ever since she'd declared her decision to face her fears and had prayed for strength, Emma had sensed an inner peace that was strong enough to convince her that those prayers had been answered.

Travis, on the other hand, was acting far grumpier. It was evident he was upset about their shopping trip. He didn't try to hide the displeasure in his expression; nor had he spoken a word since they'd driven away from the house.

Well, too bad, Emma thought. Yes, she was still concerned—for herself and for her companions—but she wasn't going to let some lowlife with a bad attitude stop her from living a semblance of a normal life. Whoever had phoned to threaten her had insisted she was keeping secrets. Therefore, if they wanted her to cooperate when she finally did recall something, they'd have to keep her safe and sound.

Rational thought brought her to the additional threats and their possible effect on her friends. The next time she had a chance to speak to her nemesis, she intended to make it very clear that if anything happened to Cleo or Travis she was *never* going to talk. Period. That scheme wasn't foolproof but it certainly had merit. Two could play the game of intimidation.

As Cleo had predicted, the parking lot of the big-box store was crowded. Travis cruised around until he found an empty space close to one of the store's entrances.

"About time," Cleo chided, climbing out with her purse and waiting for Emma to slide over and join her. "I was beginning to wonder if you were ever going to park this thing."

"I wanted to be close to the door," he replied flatly. Joining the women, he took Emma's elbow while continuing to scan the open areas for threats.

She shook off his touch, and said, "I can manage just fine, thank you." She turned to Cleo. "I want you to keep close track of everything you spend on me so I can repay you."

"That's not necessary," the older woman assured her.

"I know. But it's something I need to do to keep from feeling like a freeloader. Since I don't even have any ID, there's no way I could get credit, let alone a job. Not yet. As soon as I remember more and I'm sure it's safe, I'll go to work somewhere." She began to smile. "Maybe I'll apply here. Who knows?"

"Take your time," Cleo said with affection. "There's no hurry. You've only been back home for a couple of days. Don't expect too much of yourself."

Travis reached the automatic doors ahead of them and stood in the way so they'd stay open. "Get a move on, you two. We're too exposed out here."

"Okay, okay." Cleo jostled Emma. "Come on, girl, let's head for the unmentionable department so we can ditch Mr. Gloomy Gus."

The reference and resulting sour face Travis made, combined with her own nervous energy, was enough to make Emma giggle. She knew he had their best interests at heart and she was grateful—she simply didn't want to spend every waking moment dwelling on the negative as he seemed inclined to do.

Nevertheless, she did take stock of their surroundings and scan each passing face, just in case. Now that she'd managed to relax a bit she was getting the gut-level impression that her main enemy was a bigger, bulkier person than Blake had been. It wasn't a firm knowledge, as if she could actually picture the man, it was merely a sense of his size that she recalled as making her feel small. *And helpless,* she added, chagrined.

Determined to keep her wits about her and behave normally no matter what, Emma forced a smile for Cleo and pointed. "The department we want is back there, I think."

"Right you are." The corners of the older woman's bluish eyes crinkled and she grinned at Travis. "Where do you want us to meet you when we're done?"

He folded his arms and stared her down. "I'll be watching from a distance. Stay where I can see you."

"That's gonna be a trifle hard if Emma needs to try something on," Cleo told him. "But we'll do our best, won't we, girl?"

Nerves still tingling, her sense of humor more than a little out of kilter, she laughed and said, "Sure, we will," drawing it out for emphasis. Seeing Travis's scowl deepening only made her chuckle again.

"This is not funny," he said flatly.

"I know, I know." Emma hoped she looked penitent even though she was still fighting to keep from laughing. It was that or start to cry, since she had to relieve the tension somehow.

Pausing, she laid her hand lightly on her champion's

sleeve, feeling well-worn denim beneath her fingertips, and raised her gaze to join with his. "I do understand why you're worried, Travis. I'm not belittling you. But I can't hide all the time. I'd really go crazy if I tried to do that." She gave him a conciliatory smile, hoping he'd sense her sincerity. "Please, try to understand."

He shook his head. "I have never understood one tenth of the things you've tried to explain, Emma. Why should this time be any different?" Stepping back, he jerked his head toward Cleo. "Go on. Shop if it'll make you happy. Just don't take so long that I fall asleep on that bench over there."

Emma's grin widened and her spirits lifted even more. She was really looking forward to getting a few nice things. It was as if new clothes would be a harbinger of her new start. A new life. A fresh opportunity to find the happiness that had so far eluded her.

She might not remember many details about her quest for stardom and consequent fall into hard times and maybe even criminal pursuits, but she was certain of one thing. She had not been truly happy since the moment she had left Serenity and Travis Wright behind. That had been the beginning of the end.

And now? Turning to accompany Cleo, Emma realized why she was feeling so at peace. Travis was keeping watch. What could possibly go wrong with him right there?

Picking out an unknown person or persons from a milling crowd was not merely hard, it was practically impossible. Travis knew roughly what Blake Browning looked like but that wouldn't be much help if, as they suspected, there was more than one man chasing Emma. All one of them would have to do was distract him while the other pounced.

The hair on the nape of Travis's neck prickled. Was he

being watched? Was Emma? He swiveled to check other shoppers. Most were couples or young mothers caring for fussy youngsters while trying to accomplish their intended tasks. Seeing the children reminded Travis of the little girl Emma had remembered. Could she be that child's mother? he wondered, not for the first time.

His heart told him how much learning that would hurt, while his conscience insisted it must make no difference. Neither he nor Emma could ever go back to the carefree relationship they had once shared. He knew that as well as he knew his own name. Nevertheless, he found himself hoping for the impossible.

Cleo's short, salt-and-pepper hair was visible above the racks of clothes. So was the light blond of Emma's. It had yet to regain the sheen of health that he had once admired but Travis didn't care. He loved to look at it, anyway.

What would Emma think if she suspected his baser motives for volunteering to watch over her? Since he wasn't positive about his feelings, either, he supposed it was okay. Yes, he wanted to protect her. Absolutely. So what was wrong with enjoying the job?

Plenty. The poor woman was as befuddled as they came. Anything less than total self-control on his part was very wrong and he knew it.

"I can do this and still keep my distance," Travis vowed in a whisper. "I *will* do it."

His gaze drifted over the racks of clothing and returned to where he'd last spied the women. He could still see Cleo's darker hair but not Emma's. That was a little disturbing.

Forcing himself to delay overt action while moving to a better vantage point, Travis fought to calm his pounding pulse and keep from making a scene.

He felt a bit silly for feeling such strong apprehension. Cleo was still on the opposite side of the clothing rack and

not acting a bit upset. That meant Emma must be close by.
If he could only catch a glimpse of her...

The darker-haired shopper turned slightly. Showed Travis her profile.

His heart leaped to his throat. It wasn't Cleo!

The fitting room was so small that one customer could barely turn around in it, so Cleo had remained outside while Emma tried on several pairs of jeans and shorts with a couple of new, scoop-necked T-shirts.

"What do you think of this outfit?" Emma asked, opening the dressing room door for the fourth time and expecting to see her shopping companion.

She scowled. "Cleo?"

There was no sign of the older woman or of the salesclerk who had given them the key to the cubicle door.

Emma took a tentative step. "Cleo? Where are you?"

A quick check of the aisle where Travis had promised to wait showed that he, too, was gone.

She started to back up, seeking the supposed safety of the tiny room. Her hand was on the knob, pulling the door closed, when meaty fingers curled around the edge of the opening to stop her.

Without thinking, Emma gave the door a hard tug, smashing the man's hand.

He yowled and pulled back.

Emma finished slamming the door before she realized it couldn't be locked from the inside! All she could do was hold tight to the knob and yell for help.

She inhaled deeply, intending to scream, when the knob was yanked away and she was no longer alone in the confining space.

The burly man clamped one hand over her mouth, stifling any sound as he put his other arm around her throat from behind.

Nearly as angry as she was petrified, Emma bit him. The taste of his skin was foul. His resultant yelp, however, was sweet.

He released her and began to shake his sore hand.

Emma reached for the door.

He stopped her with a painful shove that slammed her against the dressing room wall and caused her knees to buckle. That was when she noticed that the door did not go all the way to the floor!

Instead of screaming as her instincts insisted, she flattened her stomach to the tiles, pushed behind her with bare toes, reached forward and almost shot out of the little room.

A strong hand grasped her ankle at the last instant.

Emma shrieked. "No! Let me go!"

Her nails clawed at the smooth flooring as she was dragged backward. A few more seconds and she'd have gotten away.

"Please, God," she rasped, kicking the captured leg and trying to find purchase with the other foot.

Attempting to roll over and fight back, she wrenched her knee and howled as pain shot from her toes to her hip.

Just then, a shadow passed over her.

Emma screamed again, this time loud and long.

It seemed to Travis that hours had passed, yet he knew Emma had only been out of his sight for a few moments. Critical moments.

He had been searching for either her or his aunt and had located neither when he recognized a panicky-sounding voice. A guy didn't have to be a genius to figure somebody was in trouble. He was certain he knew who.

Sounds of a scuffle took him to the ladies' fitting rooms. No customers were visible except Emma. And she was flat on the floor, looking as if she was demonstrating swimming strokes. Poorly.

So relieved he could hardly think, Travis raced toward her. He almost had hold of her wrists when she rolled halfway over and began to kick at whoever was holding her ankle.

If the dressing room door had been open, Travis would have attacked her attacker. Since it wasn't, he settled for helping Emma resist. Naturally, she fought him, too.

He kept hold and pulled her free before shoving her behind him and bracing to do battle.

Thankfully, Emma realized who he was almost immediately. She stayed close, breathing hard and struggling to speak. "Be careful, he—"

The door burst open unexpectedly. A hard body crashed into Travis with a football-like tackle and sent both him and Emma crashing to the ground.

A crowd was gathering by now, pressing in on them. People were mumbling. Several were taking pictures with their cell phones, as if witnessing an assault was newsworthy, without offering aid.

Store clerks clad in easily identifiable aprons stood nearby in a tight group.

Travis shouted, "Somebody call the police!"

Zigzagging between the milling observers, their nemesis was sprinting away.

Travis jumped to his feet, braced himself and charged into the crowd in pursuit.

Someone grabbed his arm and spun him around. He got free just as others joined in. Men and women were shouting at him. Somebody threw a punch that doubled him over. Another came from behind and draped something fabric over his head, temporarily blinding him.

"Emma!" She was his main concern. The only thing that mattered was keeping her safe. One attacker had fled, but that didn't mean there weren't accomplices.

He heard her yell, "Stop! Stop," and felt arms around

him that he knew had to be hers. She had put herself in harm's way to halt the erroneous punishment the bystanders were inflicting.

"No!" Emma shouted. "Not him! You've got the wrong man. This is my friend."

The people who had finally acted in her behalf were reluctant to release Travis, even after Emma vouched for him over and over. When the cover was finally removed from his eyes, it was evident from their expressions that they were eager to resume the chastisement, no matter who was actually guilty.

Travis shook off the last grasping hand and let his gaze travel over each angry face, hoping the attacker had tarried to watch the melee. No one looked familiar.

As the muttering crowd dispersed, he reached for his cell phone to call 911. There was no signal inside the building, meaning it was unlikely that any of the onlookers had been able to report a crime in progress, either.

"Wait," Travis shouted. "Did any of you get a picture of the guy who grabbed my friend? He ran right past you."

No one responded. Instead, individuals turned away, pretending they didn't hear or understand.

Emma gripped his arm. "Let them go. I got a good enough look at him to know it wasn't Blake. This man was much bulkier and darker. Older, too, I think."

"Will you be able to identify him if you see him again?"

"Yes. Well, probably. Right now I'm too scared to think straight." She smiled. "Meaning I'm normal, right?"

He was relieved to see her wry sense of humor surfacing. It was clearly a coping mechanism but Travis didn't care. Emma was safe. That was all that counted.

Pulling her close to his side, he ignored the lingering pain from the sucker punch and asked, "Where's Cleo?"

When Emma turned her wide, blue gaze up to him and he read the fear in it, he realized she didn't know.

"Where was the last place you saw her?" he asked, tamping down panic for Emma's sake.

"Here. I thought she was going to wait for me."

Travis took her hand and led her quickly to the other dressing rooms, rapping on each door while Emma peered under to check for occupancy. They were all empty.

"Time to notify security," he said. "Since nobody else seems to have called them."

"I'm worried about Cleo."

"So am I. Stay close."

Emma gave a weak laugh, padding along beside him barefoot. "You couldn't get rid of me right now if you tried."

As far as he was concerned, that was the best news he'd heard in days.

They found Cleo pounding on the customer service desk and trying to convince the clerks that there was a serious problem back in the fitting area. Unfortunately, she sounded so rattled her frantic pleas were being disregarded.

Hugging Emma and Travis the moment she spied them, Cleo continued to berate the staff, half weeping, half joyful and no-nonsense.

"Where were you?" Travis demanded.

"Answering the call of nature, if you must know. By the time I got back to the dressing room, there was a crowd gathered and I couldn't get through. I heard shouting so I came up here for help." She made a sour face. "Too bad I didn't get any."

Emma saw one of the workers listening to a walkie-talkie, then heard her say, "It's all right, ma'am. Our security people have checked and there's nothing wrong."

Backing up to the counter and hoisting herself into a sitting position, Emma spun on her back pockets and displayed her injured ankle. The red marks from the man's fingers were already starting to show bruising.

"In that case," she said with disgust, "maybe you can tell me how I got *this* while I was trying on clothes."

"We have no knowledge of your injury," the officious clerk declared. "It could have happened before you arrived."

"Suppose we let the Ash Flat police decide that," Travis said, producing his cell phone again. "Shall I step outside and call them or will you do it?"

Emma could have kissed him. Cleo did.

SEVEN

"I'd have screamed if those people had asked me one more stupid question," Emma said. "Let's stop on the way home and talk to the county sheriff about what happened, in case he hasn't heard."

Travis chuckled as he drove. "I thought you were sick of answering questions."

"Not the serious ones. The grilling we got in that store was dumb. They acted as if I had made up the whole story because I was trying to steal these jeans. I didn't think they were going to even give me back my old shoes."

Cleo patted her hand. "It's all straightened out now. And we paid for everything, so don't give it another thought. I'm sure they were just doing their jobs, trying to protect the store."

"I wish they had done a better job of coming up with a picture of the guy who grabbed me." She looked longingly at Travis. "Besides you, I mean."

"That's another reason we need to involve Harlan," he said. "He'll be able to request professional courtesy between Sharp and Fulton counties and get a look at the images on the security cameras. They won't show inside the dressing rooms, but you should be able to spot your attacker before he cornered you."

She brightened. "That's right! And then we'll have more to go on."

The closer they got to Serenity, the more Emma relaxed. She was coming home, in more ways than one. The town square with the courthouse in the center gave the town a homespun feel, as did the quaint shops that lined the perimeter. The flower shop and some of the others, like the bakery, had been there when she was growing up. Others had changed since her youth, yet the area retained the look and feel of old times.

Cleo pointed. "I've got me a booth in the antique mall on the corner." She grinned. "You'd be surprised to see what a flatlander will pay for genuine Ozark souvenirs. I got three whole dollars for some of those little red tobacco cans."

"Good for you."

Travis was slowing and parking on the south side of the square. "She'll try selling just about anything old that isn't nailed down. I have to watch that she doesn't tie a ribbon to Bo and put a price on him."

"Oh, hush," his aunt said, making a face. "I'm not that bad and you know it."

It delighted Emma to be included in the silly exchange. She couldn't remember the last time she had laughed and felt this lighthearted.

Closing her eyes for a few seconds, she mentally thanked God for this place and these wonderful friends.

Then she opened the door, slid out of the truck and followed Travis into the sheriff's office.

Adelaide Crowe was the only officer present. "Hello again, Emma, Travis," she said cordially. "What's up?"

"Another attack," Emma said with a telling sigh. "I sure wish I knew why so many people are acting as though there's a target pinned to my back."

The slim, dark-haired deputy picked up a pencil. "You want to fill out a report?"

"Not necessary," Travis told her. "This happened in Ash Flat so it's out of your jurisdiction. I was hoping Harlan could get a copy of the surveillance tape from the store and let Emma take a look at it, though. She got the best look at the guy before he got away."

"Did you see him, too?" Adelaide asked.

"Yes, but only for a second as he ran past me and knocked us down. I have mostly impressions of his size. He was hefty, not as big as your boss but nearly. And tall. I'm guessing at least six feet because he matched my height when he crashed into us."

"Where was this?"

The deputy's eyebrows arched higher as Travis and Emma told her the whole story, including its aftermath.

All Adelaide said in reply was, "Wow," before swiveling her desk chair to face her computer screen and keyboard.

"The sheriff is out to lunch," she told them. "I'll text him for permission, then get on this request for you. Do you want to wait? It might take a while to get the video copies you asked for."

Emma caught Travis's eye and shook her head, then said, "Cleo needs to get home and I need to be there to help her. We're… I mean, she's having company for supper tonight."

"Understood. Give me your cell number so I can let you know where we stand."

Travis looked to Emma.

She shrugged. "Sorry. I don't have a phone. I don't even have proper ID, remember?"

"I'll buy her one of those cellular units with prepaid minutes the next chance I get," Travis said.

When he started to display a lopsided smile, Emma

quickly realized why. "I suppose that will mean one of us will have to go back into that same store in Ash Flat."

"Yup." His grin widened. "I can hardly wait."

She had to laugh. "Well, I for one am in no hurry to go through that again. From now on maybe I'll do my shopping via computer."

Sobering, Travis nodded. "And you can also look for your new buddy that way. If he was associated with your old band, the way I suspect, you may be able to locate his picture the same way we found Blake's."

"I'd hold off on that for a bit," the deputy advised. "Wait till we get the store tapes. Otherwise, you may cloud your memory with unnecessary faces that will keep you from remembering clearly."

"I will *never* forget the way that man leered at me," Emma said softly. "But I'll take your advice. We'll probably be too busy fixing supper to have time, anyway."

She sensed Travis moving closer to her, felt his light touch on her shoulders, leaned into him ever so slightly as he vowed, "I'll be doing my own research into who this attacker is. And believe me, if I ever see him again, he's not going to get away."

If Emma had been alone with Travis she might have cheered and thrown her arms around his neck.

Since they had an audience, she merely said, "Thank you."

The tightening of his arm was his only reply. That was enough for Emma.

Leaving the sheriff's office, Travis insisted on stepping outside first, then hustled Emma to his truck and practically shoved her through the door on the driver's side.

"Well?" Cleo asked.

"They're working on it," Travis said. He backed up and drove away as rapidly as the speed limit would allow. "In the meantime, Emma reminded me that we have company coming and you need to get home."

Cleo snorted. "I'd clean forgotten about Samantha. Good thing I used a slow oven. That roast will cook itself just fine."

Tuning out the ensuing female conversation about the rest of the meal, Travis went over the new revelations in his mind. There were clearly at least two criminal types involved. Blake Browning, they knew. The other man they had only seen once. Travis didn't think he'd met him in the past—at least that was the impression he'd gotten in the few seconds their glances had met.

The additional feeling he'd gotten in those brief moments was one of malice and anger, both so strong that they radiated from the man's face as if he could kill with a look—or wished he could. There was no doubt he was very dangerous. And undoubtedly determined.

Pulling into the yard, Travis noted how quiet it was. Where were Bo and the other dogs? Why hadn't they gathered to greet his familiar truck?

He braked to a stop and held out his arm to restrain his passengers. "Wait. Don't get out yet. Something's wrong."

"I'll say," Cleo replied. "I know I locked that door and it's standin' wide open."

Travis slammed the driver's door and leaned in the open window. "Emma, do you remember how to drive?"

"Sure."

"Then slide over behind the wheel and get ready to floor it if trouble starts."

"I'm not leaving you."

"Yes, you are. You'll need to get Cleo to safety."

"Oh, posh," the older woman grumbled. "To listen to you, a person would think I was too ancient to defend myself. Or my family."

"I just want to check the house before anybody else goes in."

Cleo apparently had other ideas because she went right as Emma slid left and was halfway to the kitchen door before Travis caught up with her and grabbed her arm.

"Get back in the truck."

"Don't be silly. I'll be a lot safer once I get my hands on my scattergun and you know it." She twisted free and stomped up the porch steps.

As she reached into the out-of-the-way corner where she'd propped the .12 gauge, Travis put his hand on the pistol he kept above the cabinets. Thankfully, it was still loaded and ready.

"All right," he said with chagrin. "We're both armed. How about you staying here to keep an eye on Emma while I search the house?"

"Fair enough," Cleo said. She tucked the long gun into the crook of her arm to carry it safely and started back outside.

Travis heard her curdling yowl as loudly as if she'd been standing beside him with her mouth to his ear.

"Traaaaa-vis!"

He hit the porch at a run. One look told him what was wrong. The truck was just where they'd left it.

Emma was not.

Contrary to the way Travis had been acting, Emma did not have a death wish. Hands clamped tightly to the steering wheel, she had waited, as instructed. After Cleo had left the truck and she was alone, however, the reason he'd given her for staying put was no longer valid.

A shiver had shot up her spine and prickled at the roots of her long hair. She'd held her breath and strained to listen. The sound wasn't loud; nor was it familiar. It was the plaintiveness of it that had wrenched her emotions and made her slide out of the truck.

Whimpering was coming from the closed barn. She'd paused, considered making a run for the house to get help, then had decided against raising another alarm when her companions were busy searching for intruders.

It was the dogs she was hearing. They must have been shut in the barn. And since they weren't barking wildly there was probably no menace nearby, Emma had reasoned.

The closest access was mere steps away. She'd reached for the door latch. Heard it click to release.

Without a backward glance, Emma had slipped into the barn.

Travis's dogs were lying on the floor as if asleep. Only old Bo managed to raise his mottled gray-and-black head when he saw her.

She fell to her knees beside him and gently stroked his fur. "Oh, baby, what happened?"

His tail thumped weakly against the packed-dirt floor.

Emma continued to pet him as she assessed the other animals. They were breathing! Praise God!

"What did they do to you, Bo?" Her initial fear was that the friendly animals had been poisoned but then she remembered seeing a neighbor's dog get deathly ill after accidentally eating poisoned rat bait and realized that these dogs were acting differently. Their respirations were slow and steady, not rapid as if they were struggling to breathe.

Bo, who had been relaxing under her tender touch, suddenly tried to get to his feet.

Still on her knees, Emma steadied him.

He whined. Tried to walk and faltered.

That was when she heard the shouting. Someone was calling her name.

"In here!" she screamed. "In the barn! Hurry!"

* * *

The sight that greeted Travis when he burst through the door was one of pathos. There were tears in Emma's eyes as she cradled and supported his old hound. Scattered around them were the bodies of his other dogs. It took him a moment to realize they were still alive.

Braced for battle, Travis scanned the darkened corners of the cavernous structure. "What happened?"

"I don't know," Emma said. "I heard whimpering so I came to investigate."

"You were supposed to stay in the truck."

"Yes, and your dogs were supposed to be on guard. When I figured they'd been shut up in here I decided to let them out. Under normal circumstances that would have been a smart move."

"What's the matter with them?" he demanded.

"How should I know? I just got here a minute ago myself." She lowered her voice. "And stop shouting. You're scaring poor Bo."

Certain they were safe, Travis holstered the pistol just in time for Cleo's arrival. "You can put the shotgun down," he told his aunt. "Whoever did this is long gone."

She gasped and stared. "Are they all right?"

"We think so," he answered. "I'll give the vet a call just in case, but since Bo is coming around I suspect the others will, too. They're smaller than he is, so an equal dose of sedative would knock them out for longer."

Lifting the old dog in his arms, Travis straightened. "Let's take Bo into the kitchen first. I'll come back for the others as soon as we've checked the whole house."

He nodded to Emma. "You, too. And this time, follow orders."

It was clear from her closed expression that she didn't appreciate being told what to do. Travis huffed. He didn't know what her problem was. He was only trying to protect her, yet time after time she had done as she'd pleased in spite of his good intentions and sensible advice.

Cleo held the door open so the others could pass, then joined Emma with her shotgun at the ready once again.

The older woman's grit made Travis smile. Cleo was one of a kind, a true country farmwife, just like the pioneers had been.

Watching the two women precede him up the porch steps, he was struck by how similar they were—and he didn't like admitting it. Cleo was resourceful, brave, intelligent...and stubborn as a mule. No wonder she and Emma had hit it off so well. Their personalities were mirror images.

He laid Bo on a blanket in the corner by the stove before pulling out his cell phone and handing it to Emma. "Call the sheriff first and tell him we've had a break-in. Then let Cleo call our vet and fill him in, just in case we have to take the dogs in after hours."

"Do you really think they'll be all right?" Emma asked.

Her heartrending tone and somber expression reminded Travis how much she'd always loved animals. "Yes. Bo already looks better. I'll bring the others inside as soon as I've finished checking upstairs." He smiled slightly. "Judging by the look on your face, they're going to be spoiled rotten tonight."

Emma turned to Cleo. "Can they stay in? I mean, I know you're having company for supper but I feel so responsible."

"Yes," Cleo said as she propped the shotgun in an out-of-the-way corner and began to wash her hands at the sink. "We'll pen 'em up in the laundry room. In the meantime, you'd best make that call and then get busy. You have green beans to snap while I fry the bacon for seasoning."

Travis paused just long enough to give his faithful old

hound a pat on its grizzled head and listen to Emma begin her explanation to the sheriff.

Then, he drew his pistol and started upstairs.

The last thing he heard from the direction of the kitchen was Emma saying, "Yes. I was scared to death."

EIGHT

Travis finished his evening chores, then spruced himself up for supper and rejoined the women in the kitchen just as their guest arrived.

With a knock on the back door and a cheery "Hello," Samantha Rochard-Waltham poked her head in. "Hope I'm not late."

"Not at all," Travis said, pulling the door open the rest of the way and gesturing. "Come on in."

"Mmm, smells like meals Mama used to make," the nurse said. "Thanks for inviting me. On the nights when John works I usually grab a pizza and eat alone."

"I'm glad you could make it. Did Cleo explain why we asked you over tonight?"

"She did." Grinning, Samantha slipped off her coat and handed it to Travis before proceeding to the table, where Emma was putting out silverware. "Now that I see Emma again, I remember her."

"I wish I could say the same," Emma told her. "Although you do look familiar."

"There's no rush. Sometimes it's best to just take things as they come. The more you struggle to remember, the harder it may be."

"Well," Cleo chimed in, "supper's as ready as it's gonna get. Let's sit down and dig in, shall we?"

Travis helped carry the food to the table, then held chairs for the three women before seating himself. To her credit, their guest had casually joined Emma and was chatting away as if there was nothing wrong.

That's a false impression, his mind countered. *Be careful you don't fall into the trap of assuming Emma is her old self. She isn't.*

Taking such wise advice was harder than it should have been—at least that was how it seemed to him.

Emma cleared her throat. She raised her gaze to meet Cleo's, then Travis's, before looking to Samantha. "How much have you been told about me?"

"Why don't you just start from the beginning and tell your story in your own words. That way I'll be sure to get it right."

Huffing, Emma put down her fork, blotted her lips with a napkin and shook her head slowly, contemplatively. "Everything is pretty jumbled. I remember running away and being very frightened. I hitched a ride to Serenity in a semi and got out when I spotted Travis's truck at the sale barn. He brought me here, to Cleo. That's when the real trouble started."

"Let's stick to you and your memories for now," Samantha suggested gently. "Have you recalled anything about the reason you were on the run or who was after you?"

"We think there are at least two men," Emma said.

Travis agreed. "We have an internet image of one of them and the second tried to grab Emma when we were shopping in Ash Flat. Harlan is working on getting copies of the store's security footage so we can point the guy out for him."

He noted the subtle raising of the nurse's hand and realized he'd interrupted Emma's recital so he fell silent again. It was hard to watch her struggle, yet he understood the need for her to express herself without interference.

"The worst time is when I dream," Emma said. "I see a small, dark room and imagine being back there again. It makes me afraid to go to sleep." She displayed her chafed wrist. "I was handcuffed. A chain kept me from going any farther than the bathroom."

Samantha took her hand and examined the injury. "This is recent. You must not have been on the run for very long. Cleo told me you remembered hitching a ride from Tennessee. Is that right?"

"Yes. A trucker picked me up at a rest stop outside Memphis. I remember running through a forest before that. Somebody shot at me but I got away."

"Is it possible you were drugged, too?" Samantha asked. "If so, there's a chance that repeating that kind of medication, under controlled conditions, will trigger more memories."

"Really? Why?"

"No one knows." The nurse leaned back and rested her hands on the edge of the table, apparently choosing her words carefully. "There's a kind of amnesia that can occur as a protective function of the brain during intense stress or trauma and repress that experience from conscious awareness."

Travis recognized the description from one of his recent internet searches. "Dissociative amnesia?"

"Yes. It's similar to PTSD. There's a lot of controversy in the medical community about its cause and effect. Some say it's all psychological while others claim it should be studied from a biological and neurological standpoint. Those doctors insist that extreme stress, and perhaps ongoing pressure, result in widespread alterations in neurotransmission."

Emma's eyes were wide with interest. "Do you think that's what's wrong with me?"

"Maybe. I'm no psychiatrist. I do know that in many cases the problem corrects itself, particularly when the patient stops being afraid."

"That's going to be hard to do," Travis interjected, "since the criminals responsible are still harassing Emma."

"The dogs," she said, sounding excited to have thought of something. "Travis's dogs were drugged. That may have been what they did to me to keep me quiet, too."

"It might be," Samantha said. "I can write you a prescription for something mild to help you relax and sleep if you want. Then, when you think you're ready, you can try taking one tablet before bedtime and have Cleo stand by to wake you in case your memories return too vividly."

"Do you really think they will?"

Travis could tell Emma was both enthused about the chance to remember and scared of doing so. That made perfect sense.

"I don't know," Samantha said flatly. "I wish I did. Medicine is not an exact science. We give it our best guess and hope for a cure." She pointed to the ceiling. "A lot of healing is thanks to The Man Upstairs, if you know what I mean. I can't count the number of times a patient has surprised me and gotten well after doctors have given up."

"Amen to that," Cleo said. "Who's ready for dessert?"

Travis saw Emma lean closer to Samantha to say, "There's one more thing I need to mention. I keep picturing a little girl. She's looks to be about five years old and blonde with blue eyes, like me."

"Could you be picturing yourself as a child?" the nurse asked.

Although that possibility had never occurred to Travis, Samantha's next question made his blood run cold.

While Emma sat there, looking confused, Samantha asked, "Or could the little girl be your daughter?"

* * *

For Emma, the rest of the evening was a blur. She had remained polite and had tried to answer other questions while, in the back of her mind, there remained intense bewilderment regarding the child.

Could she actually be a mother? Would anybody be able to forget something that important? She would have asked the nurse that very thing if she hadn't been afraid to hear the answer. Try as she might, she could not remember a smidgen more.

Even after they had bade Samantha goodbye, cleaned up the kitchen together and retired to their separate bedrooms, Emma remained keyed up.

She closed the door behind her, kicked off her shoes and padded barefoot to the window without turning on any lights. A full moon illuminated the countryside. Lighted windows glowed in a few distant neighbors' homes. Beyond that lay the only high ground for miles around and the flashing red beacons on the pair of radio and telephone relay towers at its crest.

"I remember those!" she realized with delight. "I do. And the field trips my classes used to take up there."

She almost jumped for joy and clapped her hands. Although the urge to awaken Cleo and Travis to tell them was strong, she resisted in favor of just letting her mind wander as it had been.

The reward was instant. She was back in her teens, giggling and teasing Travis while he chased her with a handful of leaves he insisted were poison ivy.

Emma's grin widened. She could picture herself laughing and pointing to the leaves in his hand.

You're crazy! she had shouted.

I know what I'm doing, he'd replied. *This stuff never bothers me. Give me a kiss and I won't rub it on you.*

No way!

She had outrun him long enough for their FFA leader to intervene and stop the game. By the time the man had lectured Travis and had convinced him that the plant really was poison ivy rather than a look-alike, it was too late. Poor Travis had itched for weeks.

Nostalgia for the old days washed over Emma and she leaned a shoulder against the window frame. Those were good times. Happy times. And yet, she had been convinced that a better life awaited her in Music City. How could she have been so wrong?

Shivering, she wrapped her arms around herself. Bits and pieces of high-school life and her initial attempts at professional singing darted in and out of her mind. Being raised in rural Arkansas among so many bluegrass and country musicians, she had never considered any other kind of music. Well, except gospel. Going to church was so much a part of country life it rarely required mention.

She began to hum a familiar hymn, seeing herself stepping forward and raising a microphone while the rest of the choir sang backup. The image of the congregation was clear. And there sat Travis, in his usual spot in the third pew with other young adults, smiling and silently cheering her on. *Dear, sweet Travis.*

He'd joined her after that service to escort her home, as usual. The pickup he'd been driving then was barely holding together, but he'd been proud of it just the same. If she had only known...

She recalled the rush of gladness she'd felt when he'd started talking about the future, because she could already see herself performing onstage in Nashville. And then he had pulled over and done the unthinkable.

Tears spilled over Emma's lashes and slid down her cheeks as she envisioned that moment.

His earnest expression had reached into her heart and made it ache. He'd taken her hand.

Emma, I was going to wait to ask you this until I'd saved up enough to buy a little place of my own, but I don't want to lose you.

You'll never... she had started to say before he had silenced her with a gentle touch of his finger on her lips.

Hush. Let me get this out before I lose my nerve.

Nodding, she had begun to sense the portent of the moment and to guess what he was going to say. Despite all her insistence that they could be together later, after she was famous, he was going to pop the question. And there was no way she could stop him.

Travis had taken a blue-velvet-covered box from his jacket pocket and held it out to her. *I bought you a ring and everything. Marry me, Emma?*

The silence between them had seemed endless. Finally, through her unshed tears, she had done what she felt she must. She had turned him down.

"I do love you," she remembered whispering, as she repeated herself in the present.

But it wasn't enough. Not then. And sadly, not now. The stronger her love for Travis Wright grew, the more she realized he deserved better. Somehow, she had taken the wrong path and was floundering in the mire of her mistakes.

Whatever she had done, whoever she may have hurt in the past, there was nothing she regretted as much as seeing that look of hopelessness on Travis's face.

If she had not been afraid she'd awaken the others, she would have given in and thrown herself across her bed to sob away her sorrows until she was exhausted.

Instead, she splashed cold water on her face, patted it dry and opened the bedroom door, intending to raid the kitchen for a glass of milk or something else soothing.

Had it not been for the moonlight streaming through her window, she might have tripped over the sleeping gray-and-black bluetick hound curled up just outside her door.

Bo raised his head when she bent to stroke him.

"What are you doing here, old boy?" Emma whispered tenderly. "Huh? Did you know I needed a friend?"

As if answering via his actions, the dog got stiffly to his feet, stretched, walked past her and proceeded to curl up again beside her bed.

Touched, and knowing the old dog might fall off and hurt himself if she invited him to join her atop the mattress, Emma pulled a pillow and blanket onto the floor and made herself comfortable next to Bo.

"We'll just share down here," she whispered, laying an arm across his warm side and breathing a sigh of contentment.

It had already occurred to her that being made welcome at the Wright ranch could definitely be a gift from God. As she grew drowsy, she wondered if the Lord might have sent her this furry companion, as well.

Right or wrong, the notion gave her added peace.

In minutes she had drifted off to sleep.

A rumbling noise roused Emma. Clouds had drifted across the moon so there was less ambient light.

It took her a few seconds to get her bearings and remember why she was still clothed and lying on the floor.

The vibration she had sensed upon waking was coming from Bo. He was growling and staring at the closed door.

She slipped an arm around his neck and pulled him close. "Hush. Quiet."

Quivering as if getting ready to lunge, the hound never took his deep brown eyes off the door.

Now she could hear it, too. Somebody was walking in the hallway. If not for the dog, she would have assumed she was hearing Cleo or Travis. She might not know the difference in their footsteps but the wise old dog did.

Defenseless, she cast around for a makeshift weapon. Unless she planned to hit the intruder over the head with a hairbrush, she was unarmed. And so was the dog, considering his advanced age. One swift kick in his brittle ribs could be the end of the poor thing.

Emma froze, listening, staring. Was the knob turning? It looked as if it was, although in the dim light it was impossible to be certain.

Bo reacted with another growl.

She held his muzzle and hissed, "Shh."

The misplaced pillow and blanket would be sure signs that the room was occupied if someone peeked in. Therefore, she gathered them up and crawled to the opposite side of the bed, wedging herself between the frame and the wall.

To her relief, Bo followed.

She gripped his collar with one hand, the other ready to stop from making more noise.

Hinges squeaked. Peering beneath the bed, Emma saw a pair of worn hiking boots. She couldn't tell who was wearing them but they were definitely big. And dirty.

A muttered curse echoed through the silent house.

Bo gave a lunge and broke free.

With a howl that would have done his wild ancestors proud he attacked the intruder while Emma screamed, "No!" at the top of her lungs.

NINE

Travis had slept in his jeans for another night. He'd hit the floor and was moving before he even realized why he was awake.

The howling was coming from Bo. The human screams, from Emma. Why they were both raising the roof didn't matter. The woman might be having mental problems, but the well-seasoned dog was as reliable as any animal he'd ever owned. If Bo thought something was wrong, it was.

Straight-arming his way into her room through the half-open door, he saw her peeking over the top of the mattress from the far side. Before he could ask what was wrong she popped up and pointed with her whole arm. "That way! Quick. Bo's after a prowler."

"Stay there."

Travis pounded down the stairs two at a time. By the time he reached the ground floor, Bo was in the kitchen, whining and pawing the back door, while the other dogs barked from their temporary quarters in the laundry room.

It didn't take a genius to figure out that the intruder had escaped. And, unlike a couple of harebrained women he could mention, Travis was not about to go exploring in the dark and make himself a target. Again.

He'd managed to quiet all the dogs with a few calm words and slow his own pounding heart by the time Emma and Cleo joined him. Cleo was still in her robe but Emma was dressed. Come to think of it, she'd been wearing those same clothes when she'd shown herself upstairs.

If those new jeans fit her any better it would be against the law, Travis thought, taking care to keep his appreciation to himself. Emma might have lost some weight, but she was still the prettiest girl he'd ever known.

No. Not a girl. Not anymore, he admitted with a sigh. She was not only a woman, she might be a mother. Every time he allowed himself to picture her with another man's offspring it cut him to the quick. This was not the first time he had wondered if he'd be able to love Emma's daughter as much as he loved her. Perhaps, with God's help he would. On his own, he wasn't at all sure.

She pulled the oversize gray sweatshirt on over her T-shirt and clasped it closed by folding her arms. "Did the guy get away?"

"That's what Bo tells me and I have no reason to doubt him."

"He saved me," Emma said, kneeling to give the blue-tick a hug and receiving a kiss on her cheek from its wide, pink tongue. "I'd have slept through the whole thing if he hadn't woken me in time to hide."

"You were still dressed. Were you expecting trouble?" Travis asked, scowling at her.

"No. Bo showed up at my bedroom door right when I needed his companionship and I thought the least I could do was move to the floor to keep him company."

Eyebrows arching, Travis remarked, "You were sleeping on the floor?" The corners of his mouth started to twitch. "With my dog?"

"As a matter of fact, I was," Emma said, standing to face him and sticking out her chin the way she used to whenever they would argue as teens.

The lopsided grin broadened into a full smile as Travis

looked at her. If her memory recovery was half as fast as the return of her feistiness, she'd be back to her old self in no time. This was the Emma he had known and loved, not the unfortunate waif he'd found hiding in his truck mere days before.

"I'm sure Bo appreciated it," Travis drawled, "and you'll be glad to hear he's had all his shots and a recent flea-and-tick treatment, too."

"Good to know," Emma shot back. "I'd hate to have to take a bath in sheep dip."

Cleo cackled gaily and clapped her hands. "Hallelujah! You two are finally starting to sound like your old selves."

Emma sobered and the look she gave him made Travis follow suit. His eyes narrowed. "What is it? Have you remembered something else?"

"Boots," she said softly as she massaged her temples with her fingertips and closed her eyes. "The man who showed up at my bedroom door was wearing lace-up boots, like for hiking."

"Is that good?" Cleo asked.

"Yes, and no." Emma pressed her lips into a thin line before she explained. "Blake would never have been caught dead in anything but pricey cowboy boots. Our visitor must have been the guy who came after me in Ash Flat."

"Or a third man," Travis said flatly. He flipped open his cell phone. "Harlan is going to get really sick of hearing from me, but maybe this will convince him to insist on getting those in-store camera images ASAP."

"It's nearly five in the morning," Cleo said, "and I seem to be the only one who's not dressed, so I'll just run upstairs and get some clothes on. You two might as well get the coffee started. Make a full pot. If I don't miss my guess, we'll soon have plenty of company willing to help us drink it."

Travis glanced at Emma while he waited for the sheriff's office to answer his call. She had already begun to busy herself at the sink, following Cleo's orders without question. So why did she seem to have so much trouble listening to him when he made perfectly sensible suggestions?

It must be me, he reasoned, not pleased with that conclusion. He and Emma used to be so in tune it was almost as if they could each tell what the other was thinking.

That brought added color to Travis's face and he turned away to hide his reaction. Truth to tell, it was probably for the best that Emma could no longer read his mind because there were times when his thoughts were far from innocent and he didn't want her to withdraw again. When all this was over and she was her former, sensible self, then perhaps he'd tell her more about his feelings.

And if she *never* recovered? he asked himself.

That question was so unacceptable he refused to even consider an answer. All he had to do was continue to keep her safe and bide his time. Surely, that would be enough.

Watching Emma return to hug Bo again, he almost laughed when he realized he was envying the dog!

Coffee drunk, breakfast shared and explanations completed, Emma escorted Adelaide Crowe to the door. "I'll just walk her out and give Bo and the other dogs some exercise at the same time," she told Cleo and Travis. Before they had time to object she was outside with the dogs and the deputy.

While Bo galloped off with the rest of the recovered dog pack, Emma stayed close to Adelaide.

"I get the feeling there's more you want to tell me," the officer said, pausing next to her patrol car.

"In a way." Emma cast a fleeting glance back at the house to be certain they were alone. "I want to get out of here so whoever is after me will leave the Wrights alone. I thought maybe you could offer some suggestions."

"Do you have money for a motel?"

"I'm afraid not. Maybe Cleo would loan me some, but I know Travis won't. He keeps insisting I have to stay here."

"That'd be the smartest move," Adelaide said. "At least until we get a line on Blake Browning and his buddies."

"Is there more you're not telling me? It might help me remember if I had a little background on the band." Emma studied the other woman's expression. "There is, isn't there? Somebody said something about my mother wanting to locate me several years ago and Harlan telling her that some of the band members had been in trouble with the law. Is that true?"

Nodding, the deputy sighed noisily. "Oh, yeah. Big-time trouble, as in arrests for theft and drugs."

"Was I…? I mean, could I have been…?"

"We don't really know. We didn't find your name in the old files. One woman eventually confessed and was sent to prison, but it looks as if the rest of the band and the roadies went free."

"Roadies? Oh, I know what those are! The crew that sets up and breaks down equipment when we're moving from town to town." Her brow knit. "A bus. We had a tour bus!"

"Okay. Do you know what happened to it?"

"No." Her spirits fell. She momentarily closed her eyes, trying to recall details of the vehicle and its occupants. "I can picture the inside okay, and some of the instruments and such. But no people. Not even myself. It's as if I'm standing at the top of the stairs next to the driver and don't want to go any farther."

"Maybe you'd already left Browning's band because you didn't approve of their crooked dealings."

"I certainly hope so," Emma said, her cheeks warming

with embarrassment. "I can't imagine that I would have stayed if I'd known they were up to no good."

"Well, whatever happened, whoever held you against your will, they obviously want you back. Badly." She patted Emma's shoulder. "If I were you, I'd forget about leaving here for the time being and count my blessings that there are folks willing to look after me."

"I suppose you're right. Thanks for coming out again."

"Just doing my job."

"Thanks anyway," she called as the deputy waved and drove away.

Much as Emma hated the idea of exposing her friends to danger, she had to admit their presence was a godsend. Perhaps literally. And if her heavenly Father had placed her here, how could she deny His divine wisdom?

Unless this was the inevitable punishment for her sins, Emma countered. Even a person who had been forgiven might be forced to face the consequences of his or her mistakes.

If she had been a part of a group of criminals, she could very well need more than God's forgiveness. She might also have to own up to breaking the law and join the other guilty person in prison.

The notion of going to jail, particularly for a crime she could not recall, shook Emma from her toes to the top of her head and left her stomach tied in knots. If her future was truly ruined, the best thing she could do was distance herself from Travis—and his aunt—as much as humanly possible.

She had noted more than concern in his gaze when he'd looked at her lately and suspected he still cared for her, perhaps almost as much as he had when they were younger. The urge to nurture that emotional bond was strong, yet she vowed to push it aside.

He might believe he was the one protecting her, but

Emma knew that that sharp sword cut both ways. She would guard his life—and his heart—as long as there was breath left in her body.

Emma watched the patrol car getting farther and farther away and fear pricked her like the wickedly sharp thorns on the wild honey locust so prevalent in the old-growth forests.

Looking beyond the pastures and into the woods, she shivered. It wasn't what she could see that frightened her. It was what she *couldn't* see.

Her enemies were out there. Perhaps far, perhaps near. She knew it. And, in the depths of her consciousness, she knew one more thing.

They would never give up, never let her go. They would keep coming after her.

There was not a shred of doubt.

Travis continued observing Emma from the kitchen window, astounded by how courageous she was, yet worried that much of her bravado could be a result of her wanting to impress him with her ability to cope. If he had ever met anyone who was *not* coping, it was her.

Behind him, Cleo was bustling around the kitchen. She returned breakfast leftovers to the refrigerator, then pulled on a sweater and started for the door.

Travis put himself in her way. "Where are you going?"

"To collect eggs. We used a mess of 'em this morning and I want to be sure there are enough for me to bake a couple of cakes and make a meat loaf later."

"I'll go," Travis volunteered. "Emma can help me."

"Uh-huh. Who do you think you're foolin'?"

He chuckled quietly while fastening the holster to his belt once again. "Nobody. Especially not you. Let's just say I need to check on Emma and leave it at that. Okay?"

"Okay, but remember, we're still not sure she's the same

sweetheart we both once knew." Cleo handed him a small,
wire basket and gestured toward the door. "Go on. Do
whatever you have to. I trust your judgment."

"Well, you're the only one, then," Travis said wryly.
"Sometimes I feel as befuddled as Emma is."

"It'll come back to her," Cleo assured him. "The only
tricky part will be whether or not she chooses to tell us
the whole truth when it does."

"She will. I know she will. Just because she's had a
rough time lately, that doesn't mean her basic character
is different."

With that, he left his aunt and hurried to where he'd
last seen Emma. All the dogs had gathered at her feet and
were vying for attention.

"You're spoiling them rotten," he told her with a smile.

"It's more the other way around," she said. "They make
me happy by liking me so much. It's as if they know I
need friends."

"Besides me and Cleo, you mean?"

"Can't have too many friends."

"No argument there," Travis said. He held up the basket. "Come on. Cleo needs the eggs collected."

Emma's hesitation wasn't unexpected. As a matter of
fact, it gave him added hope.

"I—I don't think I like chickens," she said, frowning.

"That's another good sign. You never did take to them,
particularly broody hens that come after you to protect
their nests."

"I was right? About the chickens, I mean?"

"Sure were. You had a 4-H poultry project one year,
after I'd already moved up to membership in FFA. I'd
promised to help you with it, but as soon as those cute little chicks started to mature and act erratic, you refused to
even go into the pen with them. I had to take them to the

county fair for you, too." He held out his free hand. "Come on. I'll protect you from the killer chickens."

"Very funny."

He chuckled warmly. "I thought so."

Emma held back, tugging on his hand. "Wait."

"No excuses. Face your fears," Travis teased, grinning at her.

She raised her chin, sniffing the air. "Do you smell something strange?"

Pausing beside her, he scanned the outlying areas. Breezes were strong enough to ripple the new blades of grass among the longer, straw-colored stems left standing the previous season. Everything seemed normal. "It looks okay to me."

"I could have sworn I smelled smoke a second ago."

"Do you still smell it?"

"No, but…"

"You can look out the back door of the barn while I gather eggs if it'll make you feel better."

"I guess so." Emma smiled shyly. "As long as you're sure you have no attack chickens lurking in there."

"Nope. Not a one."

Satisfied that she'd follow him, Travis entered the barn, taking a moment to let his eyes adjust to the dimmer light. Motes of dust danced in sunbeams coming through the loft door while the land to the rear of the structure lay in shadow.

"The dogs are out back now," Emma called to him after swinging open part of the rear door. "Looks like they've found something in the grass."

He doubted it. Nevertheless, he decided to humor her. Setting aside the wire basket, he joined her and let her direct him. "Where?"

Emma pointed. "Over there. See?"

"Okay," Travis said calmly, not dreaming anything

else was wrong. "Come on. Let's see what kind of critter they've run to ground this time."

"I hope it's too early in the spring for chiggers," she said, clearly reluctant to step out with him.

"Maybe ticks but no chiggers," Travis teased, pulling her along.

All was well until they approached the dogs. A patch of grass had evidently been tamped down, similar to a sleeping nest a white-tailed deer might make. Trouble was, Travis knew that no deer in its right mind would bed down where farm dogs could easily find it.

The hair on the nape of his neck prickled. His heart began to beat faster. He listened, wishing his senses were as keen as those of his canine companions.

Several slow, purposeful strides carried him to the depression in the grass. An animal could have made it, he supposed. Unless…

Instead of growling, Bo was wagging his tail. "If I didn't know better I might think you'd brought us all out here to play a trick," he said, giving the hound a pat. "What about it, boy? Are you messing with us?"

The old dog wagged all of himself, obviously pleased to receive extra affection. Then, he put his nose to the ground and began to sniff in ever-widening circles.

Travis proceeded cautiously. He didn't expect to find anything else, he was simply going through the motions to placate Emma.

That was when he saw it. A cigarette butt lay on top of a small section of bent grass. And beside it was an open book of matches.

Travis tensed. Lifted the matchbook by its edges to look at the printed advertisement. It was for a coffeehouse. In Nashville.

Meeting Emma's eyes, he could tell she had seen enough.

Judging by the ashen color of her cheeks and her trembling hands, she knew exactly what this clue meant.

He displayed it for her. "You know this place." It was not a question.

"I—I think so. That logo looks very familiar."

"Then we have a new location to start another search," Travis told her, trying to keep the excitement out of his voice.

To his dismay, his former sweetheart looked scared to death. He cupped her elbow. "Bad memories?"

"No. That's just it," she said, her words barely above a whisper. "I had a little flash of knowledge when you first picked that up. As soon as I tried to recall more, everything vanished."

Since none of his dogs were barking or acting agitated, he felt safe enough—for the present. He took a step closer and found her doing the same, meaning he could easily slip an arm around her shoulders.

"I want to know," Emma insisted, resting her forehead on his shoulder. "I really do. I just can't seem to focus. The harder I try, the worse it is."

"Then maybe the secret is to not try so hard. Samantha said something like that, too. Remember?"

"I don't seem to have much patience."

"You never did," Travis said. "You know what they say, don't you? Never pray for patience unless you're ready for the Lord to give you plenty of reasons to wait."

"That does ring a bell." Emma glanced up at him. "Speaking of church, I'd like to go next Sunday, if that's all right with you."

"Sure. I have a concealed-carry permit and Arkansas law now allows me to take a gun into the sanctuary, so I'm not worried."

"A gun? In church? That seems so wrong."

He had to agree. "I don't intend to brandish it, if that's

what you mean. A house of worship should be safe, but there's no guarantee we won't be in danger coming or going."

Emma managed a smile. "I'll be satisfied if the church roof doesn't fall in on me when I walk through the door."

"I wouldn't worry too much. Nobody's perfect. If sinners weren't welcome in the Lord's house, the place would be empty."

"I like the way your mind works, mister." The fleeting grin she'd flashed him began to fade. "I just wish my own mind was half as clear as yours is."

And I wish my memory was dulled, Travis thought. *Then I wouldn't remember how much I once loved you. Or realize how much I still care.*

TEN

As far as Emma was concerned, she was making little progress. What she couldn't understand was why it seemed so easy for Travis to look on the bright side of everything. Surely he'd had his share of disappointments, most markedly her own desertion, yet his faith remained strong.

And hers? She simply wasn't sure. Snippets of Bible verses often popped into her head, sometimes making her think that the Lord had reminded her of them in order to comfort her. At other times, spirituality made little sense in the context of her dilemmas.

Samantha had left a prescription in case Emma wanted something to help her sleep, and Travis had filled it when he'd gone back into town to run errands. Part of her was desperate to remember everything, while another part feared that if she let down her guard she might rue what she then was able to recall.

Holding the slim, blue plastic bottle with her name on it, she actually considered throwing the medication away. Night was already a frightening time. Putting herself into drug-induced slumber seemed reckless.

Daytime, however, held far less menace. And she was already dead tired. She held up the tiny bottle. If she took one of these sedatives now and then napped for a bit, perhaps the nightmares wouldn't be so bad.

Since Travis was outside with the dogs, working, and Cleo was doing household chores, Emma figured this would be a good time to conduct her experiment. Even if she was scared silly by vivid dreams, at least she'd awaken to the sun and quickly realize she was safe and sound.

She left a note on the kitchen table that simply read, "Upstairs taking a nap," swallowed a dose with water, and went to her room.

She'd remade the bed so she merely slipped off her shoes and stretched out atop the coverlet. The pillow was soft, welcoming. Even with the blinds closed there was plenty of filtered light to warm the room and let her enjoy its ambience.

Emma sighed, waiting for the medication to take effect, and noticed only that her body felt more relaxed than usual. That notion made her smile. Almost any state would be more relaxed than she had been lately.

Sighing, she closed her eyes. Breathed slowly, deeply, steadily. Birds were singing outside her window, heralding spring and calling to their mates. "Even the birds of the air have nests," she remembered from the book of Matthew. "And foxes have holes." *I could use one of those foxholes about now. I'd just duck down and pull branches over me for camouflage.*

Camouflage?

Random shapes of mottled browns and grays danced in Emma's mind. One of the pickup trucks she had darted past during her escape had been painted that way, she realized. And those boots! They weren't merely muddy, the uppers had been done in that same, hard-to-see pattern.

Look up, her subconscious kept urging as she envisioned herself crouched behind the bed with Bo. *Just raise your eyes a little and you'll be able to see faces.*

Emma hugged herself, peeked out from behind low-

ered lashes and saw the drab walls of her former prison. She was back in that locked room. And cold. So very cold.

Shivering, she stared into the darkness and waited for what she was sure would happen. It always did. He would come. And he would threaten her again and again.

The door creaked on rusty hinges. Emma cringed back against the metal posts in the headboard of her flimsy cot. He was there, at first just a shadow, then growing in clarity until she could see his swarthy face and feel the malevolence of his presence.

"Well, I see the princess is awake. Didn't you enjoy your breakfast?"

One swift glance at the nightstand told Emma she hadn't touched the meal.

Because he drugs me that way, she realized, easing as far from her nemesis as the shackles would allow.

"Then I guess you'll have to go hungry," the burly man said. "You'll change your tune soon enough or starve to death."

"I'd rather starve than eat anything you'd touched," she shrieked. "You filthy..."

He waggled a thick finger at her. "Now, now, how would it look if folks found out our star gospel singer talked like that. Shame on you."

Gospel singer? Was that what she was?

Music drifted on the air, its charm pulling at her and taking her further into her muddled memories. Away from the makeshift prison.

Church? Yes! She was standing before a small congregation, most of whom were seated so close she could see their individual faces. Some were smiling. Others appeared emotionally affected—in a good way.

She held a microphone with foam covering the pickup to eliminate background noise. Her heart was full of love and thankfulness. A sense of euphoria washed over her.

Her voice rose in a crescendo of praise to her heavenly Father and His blessed Son, Jesus.

Emma wanted to laugh and cry at the same time. This was the life she'd been made for. The culmination of her lifelong dream to sing for appreciative audiences and use her God-given gift.

Applause followed her last note. Blinking back tears of thanksgiving, she nodded to the spectators, then politely turned and held out her arm to give credit to the musicians backing her up.

Her jaw went slack. There they were. All of them. Blake was on the acoustic guitar, a slim clone of him plucked a Dobro, and the man standing next to the bass fiddle was the same one who had kept her locked up.

Astonishment overwhelmed her. She tried to scream. No sound came. The scene began to fade as panic filled her.

Wait! There was one more person in the band. A fairhaired woman in the rear held a mandolin and there was a banjo propped behind her, as if she played both.

Emma tried to catch the woman's eye and failed. She dropped the mic and waved her arms, attempting to shout a warning.

It was no use. The young woman's eyes never left Blake and the bass player. There was abject terror in her expression, a terror Emma could certainly identify with.

Thinking that perhaps she could jump into the audience and thereby escape, Emma pivoted. They were gone. She was alone with the others—and with her fear.

As she tried to leave the stage, someone grabbed her arm. His fingers clamped so tightly it made her cry out.

"Let me go!"

"No way, darlin'," Blake Browning drawled. "We're all in this together, remember?"

Remember? That word rebounded inside her head as if she were in an echo chamber. She did remember, at least some things, and they were far from pleasant. She'd just discovered that members of their group made a practice of robbing the churches and theatrical groups that invited them to perform. The only time they'd apparently refrained from lining their pockets was when they happened to be playing in a less reputable establishment. Then, the bass player and Blake and the other guitarist, his brother, Ben, would peddle drugs. She knew that as surely as she knew her own name.

"I'm quitting and going home," Emma remembered declaring. "You can't stop me."

But they had, hadn't they?

She thought she heard sirens in the distance. Were the police finally going to arrest Blake? She certainly hoped so. Her anonymous letter to local authorities must have finally found its way into the right hands!

In the background, people were shouting but all Emma could see was the hatred in the eyes of the horrible man who was restraining her. He flung her across the dressing room. She hit the wall with a sickening crash and slumped to the floor.

Colored lights flashed behind her closed eyelids, their brilliance painful.

She tried to raise her hands, to cover her stinging eyes. Something was stopping her.

Looking down, she saw her wrists were encased in silvery handcuffs. Someone was shouting orders. Pushing her ahead. The mandolin player was there, too.

Emma met that woman's terrified gaze and suddenly realized they were friends.

"Take care of Sissy for me," the woman whispered. "Please! There's no one else I can ask."

"But...how?"

Police cars faded away. People vanished as if a thick fog had risen and covered the entire scene.

*Not seeing anything clearly was far worse than being
able to discern even the most problematic situation.*

*Emma twisted and struggled against the restrictions
of the hand that was grasping her arm. She wanted to
scream. She gulped in enough air, but when she tried to
shout, nothing happened.*

*"I'm Emma Lynn Landers," she declared. "I'm inno-
cent. Let me go? Please?"*

*The entire room began to vibrate as if she'd been over-
taken by an earthquake. Emma tried to brace herself. To
keep from tumbling into the yawning abyss that was opening at her feet.*

*Her balled fists connected with a firm surface and she
pictured herself beating on the chest of a police officer as
she and her companions were about to be carted off to jail.*

"Emma," someone called from far, far away.

*"No, no," she wailed. "I'm not guilty. I didn't know.
Honest, I didn't."*

*Bright light continued to flash. Emma squeezed her eyes
tight against the intrusion, wanting desperately to linger
in limbo long enough to understand what she'd been vi-
sualizing.*

The moment she entertained that thought, she realized
she'd been dreaming.

Her eyes popped open. It wasn't Blake or the police who
had been grasping and shaking her. It was Travis.

And she wasn't in Tennessee anymore. She was back
in Serenity.

Out of breath and still a tad disoriented, Emma looked
into his face and saw so much concern it astounded her.

"It worked. I—I remembered more," she told him.

Travis pulled her closer. "Hush. You're safe now."

She pushed away just enough to meet his gaze. "Listen so you can help me recall this later, in case I forget."

"All right."

"I was singing with Blake. And the man who tried to grab me in the store was in the band, too. So were a couple of others. One was a young woman who played a mandolin. We were all being arrested and she told me to take care of something."

"What?"

The details were already fading. Emma held her breath and forced her thoughts back to the scene of the police encounter. "She said Sissy, I think. Do you suppose that's the little girl's name?"

"We can try to find out. What else?"

"Blake, his brother, Ben, and the bass player were crooked, all right. Just like everybody thought. What I don't understand is why they didn't go to jail for their crimes."

"And why they're apparently after you," Travis added.

Emma sighed. Her shoulders slumped and she leaned against his chest, listening to his rapid pulse. "I didn't see anything about that, except right when I first fell asleep," she said with chagrin. "But we do know one important thing."

"What's that?"

"The prescription works. It relaxes me enough that my subconscious can break through."

"You're not going to put yourself through that kind of ordeal again," Travis said flatly.

"I have to," she insisted. "Because now I know for sure that somebody else needs me."

"Do you think this Sissy may be your daughter?"

"No. I got the distinct impression she belonged to the woman in my nightmare. Otherwise, why would she beg me to look after her when she was being arrested?"

Stiffening and pushing herself away so she could stand and pace the floor, Emma kept searching for more memory clues. All she could come up with was a distressing thought she'd had before.

"I left her behind," she confessed, wide-eyed. "As soon as I know where I was when I ran away, I have to go back for Sissy. I simply have to."

Travis's instant protestations fell on deaf ears. Emma had failed a friend, and probably a child, as well. She might not be able to reclaim the wasted years, but she could at least put something about them right.

She could—she would—rescue Sissy.

Somehow.

Travis wished with all his heart that he could spare Emma more anguish, yet he knew she'd never be satisfied until she remembered every detail.

"Did you actually visualize the little girl this time?" he asked gently.

She shook her head, sighed and used her fingers to rake back her long hair as she paused to gaze out the window. "No. I was onstage with the band."

Travis saw her countenance soften when she turned back to face him and said, "I was singing a gospel number."

"You always did have a special talent for that."

"Thanks." She squeezed her eyes closed, her forehead wrinkling from intense concentration. "Blake and his brother, Ben, were both on guitars. The bass player was the big guy who came after me in the store."

"And there was another woman?"

Emma's eyes glistened. "Yes. She was about my age and acted really scared, particularly around Blake."

"Go on."

"That's all there was. Well, except for the band being arrested right after the performance. That was when the female mandolin player begged me to look after Sissy."

"Okay. Let's go see what we can find in online news-paper archives for that time period."

With Emma preceding him, he followed her down the stairs. "I'm guessing you envisioned something that happened before your dad passed away. That fits with Harlan's information about the band in general, although he said the police reports didn't mention you by name."

"That's another puzzling thing," Emma said. "If I was arrested with the others, why isn't my name on record?"

"And why did your woman friend end up pleading guilty and serving time when you and the others went free?"

He saw Emma's jaw drop, her eyes widen. "Robbie. Her name was Robbie!"

"Are you sure? That sounds more like a guy's name."

"It must be a nickname."

"Okay." He gestured toward the cluttered spare room on the ground floor that he used for an office. "I'll give you the laptop while I use the computer at the desk. Between the two of us we should be able to find news reports about her arrest and conviction. If we draw a blank and have no other choice, we'll ask Harlan." He flashed a lopsided smile. "I just hate to call him again."

"He's supposed to have that store video for us to look at soon, anyway," Emma reminded him. "If we don't have anything to show for our efforts by then, we can mention it when we're in his office."

"Good plan." Watching her, he felt his anxiety slowly lessening. She was coming along well, according to Samantha's predictions and the research he'd done on his own. Yes, she had been involved with criminals, but that didn't mean she was of the same mind. Plus, she hadn't gone to jail. That had to count in her favor.

As he seated himself at the keyboard and began his search of Nashville news archives, he was reminded that

Blake Browning, Blake's brother, Ben, and the bass player had also gone free. Only the one woman had been convicted. And, given those men's current activities, there was no doubt they were as guilty as anyone. Perhaps more so.

Therefore, there was a lot more to this whole mess than they knew. There had to be. And he would find out what. Failure was not an option. Emma's life might very well depend upon his efforts.

ELEVEN

Emma's internet search turned up the first clue. She gasped and pointed to the screen. "Here! Look."

As Travis leaned over her shoulder to read the caption under the photo and begin to scan the print, she realized she should have moved farther away before calling it to his attention. The warmth of his breath tickled her cheek and his presence in her personal space was overwhelming.

Nevertheless, when he did straighten and back away, she missed his closeness.

"That explains a lot," Travis said pensively. "Your friend Roberta was married to Blake. It doesn't mention a child but that assumption also makes sense. If Sissy was hers and Blake's, as some of your previous memories indicated she might be, then Robbie would have plenty of reason to worry."

Emma was hardly able to believe her eyes. "It says she confessed to everything and exonerated the rest of the band. That's crazy. My impression of her is exactly the opposite. She was a sweetheart, not a criminal. If anybody's guilty of theft and messing with drugs it's Blake and the other guys."

"What about you? There's no mention of you at all. If you were arrested, there should at least be something."

"I know, I…"

The images of the police raid were like a vapor, yet Emma managed to grasp a bit more. Blake and his brother were shouting obscenities while the hefty bass player used his enormous instrument as a weapon, swinging it at the officers and knocking them aside until they finally managed to subdue him.

She had been put into a different police car than any of the others before having her cuffs removed by the policewoman seated next to her.

Sorry to have to do that to you, the officer had told her. *We didn't want the others to know where the tip came from.*

Emma stared at Travis. "I was the one who turned the others in," she said softly, hardly believing her memory. "That's why I wasn't booked and why my name never showed up as part of the gang after the raid."

"That's good news—isn't it?"

"Yes, and no," Emma told him as her thoughts spun. "What I can't understand is why Robbie went to jail and the men got off. I'm sure that wasn't how it was all supposed to end."

He once again leaned over her and pointed. "Read that paragraph at the bottom. It says she did confess."

Emma could hardly believe her eyes. "Why would she do that? She was no more a part of Blake's criminal activities than I was."

"How can you be positive?"

"I don't know, but I am," Emma admitted with a shake of her head. "All I remember is being shocked, just the way I am now, and thinking that the authorities had gotten it all wrong."

"I wonder if there's some way you can visit her in prison and find out more?" Travis asked.

Cold dread coursed through Emma as if ice water had infiltrated her veins. Prison meant confinement, just like the room in which she'd been held against her will. The

A SERIES OF LOVE INSPIRED NOVELS!

GET 2 FREE BOOKS!

Plus, receive
TWO FREE BONUS GIFTS!

We'd like to send you two free books from the series you are enjoying now. Your two books have a combined cover price of over $10, but are yours to keep absolutely FREE! We'll even send you two wonderful surprise gifts. You can't lose!

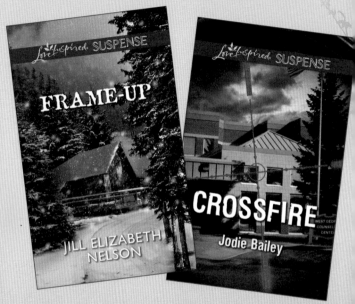

Each of your FREE books is filled with joy, faith and traditional values as men and women open their hearts to each other and join together on a spiritual journey.

FREE BONUS GIFTS!

*We'll send you two wonderful surprise gifts, worth about $10, **absolutely FREE**, just for giving our books a try! Don't miss out — MAIL THE REPLY CARD TODAY!*

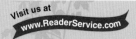

GET 2 FREE BOOKS!

HURRY!
Return this card today to get 2 FREE Books and 2 FREE Bonus Gifts!

▼ DETACH AND MAIL CARD TODAY! ▼

YES! Please send me the **2 FREE books** and **2 FREE gifts** for which I qualify. I understand that I am under no obligation to purchase anything further, as explained on the back of this card.

2 FREE BOOKS

❏ I prefer the regular-print edition
123/323 IDL GEKD

❏ I prefer the larger-print edition
110/310 IDL GEKD

FIRST NAME   LAST NAME

ADDRESS

APT.#   CITY

STATE/PROV.   ZIP/POSTAL CODE

LIS-714-IVY13

⚜ HARLEQUIN READER SERVICE — Here's How It Works:

BUSINESS REPLY MAIL
FIRST-CLASS MAIL   PERMIT NO. 717   BUFFALO, NY

POSTAGE WILL BE PAID BY ADDRESSEE

HARLEQUIN READER SERVICE
PO BOX 1867
BUFFALO NY 14240-9952

NO POSTAGE
NECESSARY
IF MAILED
IN THE
UNITED STATES

mere idea of purposely going to another place like that made her sick to her stomach and weak in the knees.

"There has to be another way," she breathed, her words barely audible. Bile rose in her throat, the taste bitter on her tongue. She knew she must have done all she could for Robbie at the time because that was her way. She would never have abandoned a friend in need.

So what had gone wrong? Apparently, plenty. Robbie had been convicted and the others had escaped punishment. Whoever had said justice was blind had been correct. The question now was why were Blake and the bass player hounding her? And why had they kept her prisoner for however long it had taken to break her spirit and affect her mind?

That thought made her mad enough to dispel the feelings of nausea. Those evil men had probably framed poor Robbie as well, and were now seeking vengeance against Emma and her Serenity friends.

"The man on the phone. The one who called the house?"

Travis nodded sagely. "What about him?"

"He accused me of keeping a secret. Do you suppose I do know something important, maybe something that can free Robbie and give her back her little girl?"

"If you did, wouldn't you have acted before she went to jail?"

"I thought I would have." Emma once again eyed the newspaper story filling the computer screen. "Look at this date. Is it possible I was already Blake's prisoner by the time Robbie was sentenced?"

"That might fit. But why is he bothering you now? If he locked you up to keep you from coming forward to testify on behalf of your friend, why continue to hound you? The trial is in the past."

"It has to be the secret, whatever it is," Emma speculated. "I'd first thought it might be something about Robbie's innocence. Now, I'm not so sure. As you said, it's too late to help her."

"Unless she recants her confession and you vouch for her during an appeal," Travis ventured. His brow furrowed. "That still doesn't explain why Blake and his buddy are so determined to make you talk, unless you really do know something else that could land them in jail—or worse."

Emma shivered and folded her arms against the unexpected chill. "I wonder if they killed someone."

"That might have been dramatic enough to affect your memory, particularly if you witnessed it."

"It would explain a lot."

"Only if it really happened," Travis warned. "I don't like those guys any better than you do, but if you start accusing them of committing murder you may put yourself in more danger than you're in already."

"Yeah. Okay. You're right."

He arched a brow. "I beg your pardon?"

"I said, you're right."

"I know what you said," he teased, "I'm just having trouble believing I heard correctly."

She had to smile in spite of her anxiety. "I'm certain I must have told you that you were right about something, sometime."

"Not lately," he said with an easy drawl. "I'd better make a note of this so I can remind you the next time you decide to ignore my advice and go off on a tangent."

A strong need to defend her actions arose. "The trip into the field to look for you was Cleo's idea. So was shopping."

"What about when I told you to stay in the truck and you ended up in the barn with the dogs?"

She grimaced. "That was a special situation. I heard whimpering and I was worried about them."

The light weight of his hands on her shoulders was reassuring yet unsettling at the same time, especially when he began to gently knead her knotted muscles.

"And I worry about you," Travis said. "All the time. There's no way I can continue to protect you if you don't listen to my advice."

"What I should do is leave here so you won't have to do anything," Emma countered. "I've already spoken to Adelaide about it but she recommended I sit tight. At least for a while."

"Excellent advice." He continued to touch her, but the massaging movement of his hands had stilled the moment she'd mentioned leaving.

"I'm not so sure. If I were gone, and Blake knew it, maybe he'd back off and stop threatening you and Cleo."

"And maybe he'd still come after us *and* you. As long as we stick together we can help each other stand against him and his cohorts. If you were alone, he'd have the advantage." Travis's voice dropped lower and sent tingles up her spine when he added, "And if he manages to get his hands on you again, he might very well lock you back up in the room you described. Are you willing to chance that?"

All Emma could do was shake her head. The idea of once again being Blake's prisoner was so appalling it was beyond imagination. She could not go back there. She'd die if he recaptured her. Emma couldn't leave Sissy with him, either. She would call the sheriff that evening and tell him what she'd remembered about the girl.

At that moment, any expectations of a happy, peaceful future vanished. She wasn't planning to knuckle under. She was simply unable to imagine anything past the final, face-to-face encounter she and Blake Browning must surely have.

God willing, I'll best him, Emma mused while butterflies beat their wings against her insides and her heart raced. *And I hope no one else is harmed when it happens.*

That was the scariest part of the entire scenario. If someone dear to her, or even a stranger, had to suffer as a result of her mistakes and inadequacies, it would magnify her sins immeasurably. That must not happen.

She squeezed her eyes shut to pray, "Please be with us, Father."

From behind her she heard Travis's softly spoken "Amen."

That was enough to bring tears. Emma sniffled and held them back. There had been altogether too much weeping going on lately. Being confused and frightened was no reason for her to cry at the drop of a hat. Or, in this case, at the innocent touch of a special person's hand and his heartfelt "amen."

Tomorrow was Sunday, as Cleo had recently reminded her, and as long as the family was still planning to attend services, Emma wanted to go, too.

Although Travis had teased her about agreeing with his opinions, he had made perfect sense when he'd reminded her that there was safety in numbers. Recalling Blake's former life, before they'd left Serenity, she knew he had never darkened the door of a church. As a matter of fact, he had belittled her love of gospel songs until he'd seen that their audiences liked them, too, particularly when she sang her favorites.

It would be good to be back among the Lord's people, Emma concluded easily. And good to raise her voice in praise once again. Perhaps, for the hour or so that she, Travis and Cleo were safely seated in the familiar sanctuary, she'd be able to lay aside her burdens and finally feel free of the heavy sadness she'd borne for longer than she could remember.

The mere notion of returning to church lifted her spirits immeasurably. Coming home to Serenity and Travis had been part of her spiritual and physical journey. Going back to the Lord's house would be another important step in the right direction.

Surely, He would bless that, she reasoned logically. The prodigal son had been welcomed home by his earthly father. How much more must God rejoice when one of His errant children returned to the fold?

Emma purposefully closed the laptop and pushed away from the side of the desk where she'd been working. They knew a lot more now than they had yesterday. By tomorrow, perhaps she would have recalled even more.

God, help me to accept those memories, no matter what they tell me or how much they hurt, she prayed silently.

That was the key, wasn't it?

She feared more than Blake and his cohorts.

She feared the reality buried in her own mind.

Travis didn't usually wear a suit jacket to church. Neither did most of the men in attendance. In this case, however, he made an exception and donned a suede blazer over his best jeans and good boots.

Poor Emma had fretted about not having proper clothing until Cleo had rummaged around and found her a denim skirt to borrow. Travis didn't recall seeing that skirt on his aunt, which was just as well, since there was no comparison between her and Emma other than an apparently similar size. On Emma, anything looked great and the skirt was no exception.

She twirled to show him. "How's this?"

"Fine. You could wear your regular jeans to Serenity Chapel if you wanted to. We don't look down on anybody, no matter how they're dressed."

"I know. That's one of the things I've always loved about worshipping there. It's as if Jesus were setting the example of loving everybody."

"Exactly." He fisted his keys. "Ready?"

"Isn't Cleo coming with us?"

"She'll meet us there after she picks up a couple of other older ladies who no longer drive. They could take the church bus but they prefer to ride with Cleo." He chuckled quietly and cupped his hand at the side of his mouth to add, "That way they can gossip privately."

"Do you think anybody has heard about me being back?"

"Undoubtedly. Nothing much escapes notice in a small town. You should know that. You grew up here."

"I know. I was just hoping…."

"Don't worry about it, Emma. People will be glad to see you no matter what. You've been missed."

"I have?"

"Yes, you have," Travis told her. Growing solemn, he added, "Especially by me."

The closer they got to the familiar church building, the more Emma began to feel at home. Other parts of Serenity had given her a sense of déjà vu but making this trip on a Sunday morning seemed so natural, so right, she had to smile.

"I'm glad we're doing this," she told Travis.

"So am I."

Beams of sunlight broke through scattered clouds and bathed the white steeple in gold as if bestowing a heavenly benediction. It seemed to Emma that God was visibly blessing her return and warming her wounded heart. This day might be one of a thousand others, but it was so special to her she could hardly contain her joy.

When she'd returned to Serenity she'd been trying to come home, yet some element of the experience had still been missing. This was it. Going to church with her best friend, and so many folks she'd known in the past, was like getting a welcoming hug from the whole community.

"I can't believe how good I feel this morning," Emma

said with a grin. "I can almost believe we've gone back to the days before I left."

To her chagrin, Travis didn't echo her sentiments. When she looked at his profile she could see the muscles in his jaw clenching.

"I'm sorry. I shouldn't have said that."

"It's okay. I only wish we could go back."

"I wish we could, too. It's just so hard to anticipate the future when you're a teen. We were kids, Travis. At least I was. All I could see was the glitter and excitement of possible success as a singer. I didn't realize I was already a star here in Serenity."

"I don't begrudge you the chance to go to Nashville," he said flatly. "I never did. What hurt the most was the way your letters changed. You changed. And then you stopped writing altogether."

A startling notion popped into her head. "Wait. When was that?"

"About the time your father passed away."

"Then it was close to the time the whole band got arrested." Emma grew pensive. "I have an idea that I may have stopped writing to you because Blake had already locked me up."

"I'd thought of that. But what about before? You sounded as if you didn't want to share your successes with me anymore. When you first went to Nashville you told me everything."

"Everything good, you mean." She sighed audibly. "By the time the band got into so much trouble we'd fallen on hard times. I didn't want anybody to be able to say, 'I told you so,' so I didn't admit we'd failed."

"What about the thefts and drugs?" Travis asked as he wheeled into the driveway leading to the church parking lot. "When did you tumble to what they were doing and turn them in?"

"I'm not sure. I remember a police officer telling me I was free to go because I'd given them the tip that led to the arrests, but I'm not positive about the timing. I know I'd never have tolerated them breaking the law once I'd found out about it."

"That says a lot for your character," he offered.

"Maybe. But it's not much of a boost to my ego to think that I was blind to it for who knows how long. If I hadn't been so trusting, maybe all this could have been avoided."

"And maybe, if you hadn't been involved, they'd still be out there robbing innocent people."

Emma had to agree. "Okay. I'll buy that. What I still don't understand is how Robbie ended up in jail."

As he parked and got out to circle to her door, Emma was able to see the concern in Travis's expression.

"One day at a time," he said as he helped her out. "I think it would be best if you stopped dwelling on the things you don't know and concentrated on the service for a change."

"Right again," she said with a smile. "I suppose now you're going to get a swelled head."

"That is twice you've admitted I was right." He mirrored her grin. "But I'll try to remain humble."

"You do that." Emma's spirits were so lifted she wondered if her feet were actually touching the ground. This was where she belonged. In Serenity. Going to church. With Travis Wright.

Beyond that lay circumstances over which she had no control. Letting those cares go and worshipping fully was all she wanted at that moment.

Later, when they went home again, she'd have plenty of time to worry.

And, God willing, to remember even more.

TWELVE

The atmosphere inside Serenity chapel was as welcoming as ever, putting Travis more at ease. He'd known in his heart that the congregation had an overall loving nature; he'd simply needed extra confirmation that those who remembered Emma would treat her as a returning sister.

They not only did that—a local reporter spotted her and begged for a story while the music director shook her hand vigorously and invited her to sing an unplanned, special song during the service.

To Travis's relief and delight, Emma blushed and agreed to sing, although a bit reluctantly.

That meant it was more advantageous for them to choose a pew near the front, making Emma visible to anyone who had not noticed her before. When she stood during the service to make her way to the raised platform in front of the choir, everyone applauded.

She picked up the microphone. Her gaze briefly roamed the dimly lit sanctuary before settling on him. He smiled and gave her a thumbs-up.

A piano and organ duet played the intro to "How Great Thou Art," a well-known hymn he remembered was a favorite of Emma's.

The moment she began to sing, it felt as if the entire building was holding its breath. Her voice was not merely beautiful, it was inspired in a way he had never noticed before. A spotlight made her blond hair glisten like spun gold. Her eyes sparkled with the emotion behind the words she was singing.

Travis folded his hands and prayed silently for her full healing. If this performance was any indication of her superbly honed talent, it was a wonder she had not found the fame she'd sought. Maybe, given another chance, she would.

That notion settled in his heart and made it ache. He had been wrong when he'd tried to keep Emma in Serenity. To have done so would have meant denying her gift, a gift that had never been more evident than it was at that very moment.

At the final crescendo, she bowed her head as if giving thanks, then looked up—and froze.

In spite of the thunderous applause, Emma looked petrified. Why? Surely she wasn't disappointed in such a stellar performance.

She began to back up, looking quickly from side to side before thrusting the mic at the choir director and hurrying off via a side door.

Astounded, Travis was a few seconds slower in responding. By the time he'd jumped to his feet to follow her, Emma had disappeared.

Raising her voice to praise God had brought Emma an unexpected elation. She'd almost forgotten what a blessing it was to open her heart and sing like that.

Tears of gratitude had blurred her vision. She'd blinked them away and stepped back, intending to rejoin Travis in the pew near the front.

Her misty gaze had drifted over the congregation. Many were getting to their feet to show their support and appreciation.

Because of that, Emma almost missed a different kind of movement from the double doors at the rear of the sanctuary.

Having an usher hold the door open for a latecomer wasn't unusual, but seeing a large, shadowed figure pause in the opening and focus only on her, was.

Although she was far from certain that the person she spied was her enemy, his arrival and subsequently menacing pose were enough to spur her to take evasive action.

The building's basic configuration had not changed since she'd been gone. The closest passageway led to the ladies' restroom and the choir room, then on to the exits on either side of the rear addition. Any of those avenues would suffice.

What she was *not* going to do was stand there in the spotlight and take the chance that her enemies would defile the service. Or recapture her.

Without a backward glance she'd turned on her heel, shoved the mic at the surprised-looking choir director and taken off at a run.

The entire service was being broadcast all over the building for the sake of those whose volunteer jobs kept them busy elsewhere, such as in the case of the nursery workers.

Emma could hear everything. Unfortunately, she could not differentiate between the sounds coming from the joyful choir and congregation and anyone who might be chasing her.

She emerged into a rear hall that formed the crosspiece of a T-shape. "Which way? Which way?" Her panicky words were little more than a ragged breath.

No divine guidance was forthcoming. The urge to pause and pray was overridden by fear.

Stay or go?

Neither choice seemed right. If she stayed she might be

putting many others in danger. If she fled to the outside, where could she hide?

And what about Travis? He was armed, yes, but she had left him behind. Where would he be most likely to come looking for her?

Emma's feet made the ultimate decision. She sped toward the glass exit door that was closest and headed for a morning greeter who had not yet left his post.

Straight-arming the door before the astonished man could open it for her, she hit the gravel lot at a run and picked up the pace even more.

A line of clear windows along the side of the building would do her no favors, she realized. Anybody who chanced to look out would be certain to see her. To know where she had headed.

Nevertheless, she kept on course until she could duck behind a row of parked cars. Once there, she leaned over, hands on her knees and gasped for air. It wasn't only the race that had left her so breathless, it was the thought that no place was safe.

Not even church on a sunny Sunday morning.

Travis left through a different door rather than call even more attention to Emma by invading the stage and using the same exit she had. He knew the hallways connected behind the baptismal area so that was where he headed.

He had no idea what had frightened her but he could not—he would not—dismiss her concerns. Even if her reaction had been no more than stage fright she needed him right now. And, truth to tell, he was desperate to make sure she was okay. Anything else was secondary.

God would understand why he'd had to jump up and follow Emma, Travis reasoned logically. Given the fact that she was nowhere to be seen, he certainly hoped the Lord would help him locate her, too.

Where? Which way?

He stood at a corner and pivoted, scanning the nearly deserted hallways in both directions. Someone was manning a side door, so Travis headed over to ask the usher if he had noticed Emma.

The closer he got, the more Travis's heart pounded. There was something wrong. Instead of greeting him as he'd expected, the older man was leaning against the jamb and holding his head.

Travis clasped his bent elbow. "What happened?"

The graying head shook slowly. "Beats me. I was just standing here, watching a lady run off, when somebody else pushed me down."

"What lady? What did she look like?"

"Blonde, I think. Youngish. I didn't get a real good look at her."

"What about the guy who shoved you?"

"Didn't see him good at all. Just kind of a blur as he ran past."

Noticing another usher approaching, Travis motioned to him to help the shaken man, then darted out through the same door.

Except for a few late arrivals, the parking lot lacked pedestrians.

Travis knew that racing around like a June bug on a hot sidewalk was stupid. So was standing still when Emma might be in terrible jeopardy.

The more the morning's events coalesced in his mind, the more certain Travis was that Emma had seen someone she'd recognized and feared. That had to be the reason she'd fled. But how was he going to locate her before it was too late?

Since they were now outside, he decide to chance calling to her. "Emma!"

She didn't answer or show herself.

Three rows down, near where he had parked the farm truck, however, someone straightened and pivoted.

It was the creep from the attack at the store! It didn't take a genius to figure out the guy was tracking Emma again.

Fighting to breathe noiselessly, Emma crouched behind a pickup truck, afraid to run farther and take a chance on being spotted, yet just as afraid to sit still and eventually be discovered.

One decision was easy. No matter what, she was going to stay as far away from other people as possible. Those who happened to be arriving late for the morning service were having to park farther behind the church so she vowed to avoid that area at all costs.

Working her way past bumper after bumper, Emma heard someone call her name. Travis! Did he know why she was hiding? Or had he followed simply because she'd run away? If he was unaware of the danger, he might make a wrong move and be injured—or worse.

What could she do? If she revealed her position to Travis, the thug would surely spot her, too.

A name to go with the swarthy face popped into her head. "Jet." The others had called him Jet and had made zooming engine sounds, joking that the nickname fit perfectly because he was always high and fast.

Would that be enough info for the sheriff to figure out who he really was? Emma wondered. Maybe, maybe not. Right now her biggest problem was not his identity—it was his proximity.

Another loud "Emma!" echoed across the parking lot. She chanced a peek over the tailgate of a nearby pickup and spotted both Travis and her nemesis. They were staring at each other.

Travis reached behind his back for his concealed weapon.

Jet didn't have to. He already had a gun in his hand.

Everything seemed to be happening in slow motion. Both men tensed and aimed.

Emma screamed, "No!"

The guns fired almost simultaneously.

She ducked and dropped to her knees before the echoes faded. There were no words in her mind or heart for prayer or for anything else.

Debilitating shock wrapped its clinging arms around her, covering her like a thick, heavy blanket and blotting out reality.

Darkness encroached at the fringes of her vision. Bright, colorful lights flashed behind her closed eyelids.

Emma thought she heard her name again and willed herself to move, to rise and respond.

Her legs were made of concrete, her arms of lead. The desire to shout never made it past her constricted throat and closed lips.

All she could envision was Travis, falling wounded, perhaps mortally. And it was all her fault. Everything was. She had brought this evil to Serenity and was helpless to stop its destruction.

At that moment of utter despondency and desperation, she imagined that even God had deserted her.

"Over here!" Travis shouted, waving his arms.

Several off-duty Serenity police officers, regular members of the congregation, had responded to the sounds of shots being fired. Ushers had followed their orders and kept the rest of the worshippers inside and safe.

The first man relieved Travis of his gun. "You hurt?"

"No. He missed me. I heard a scream and turned just as he shot at me."

"Did you shoot him?"

"I don't think so. My aim was too far off." He raised an

arm to point. "The guy ran that direction but I doubt you'll catch him. I imagine he had a getaway car waiting nearby."

"Sounds pretty far-fetched to me," the officer said.

"It won't if you call Sheriff Allgood," Travis countered. "He knows all about this mess."

"Okay. You stay put while I radio Dispatch."

"Sorry." Travis was already moving away. "There's a woman hiding out here who needs my help. I'm going to find her, with or without you."

"No way." The officer's palm was resting on the butt of his sidearm.

Travis didn't figure the man would shoot a local, at least not without plenty of provocation. "I'll stay where you can see me if I can. But I'm going."

Without a pause he began to jog down the aisles of the lot. There were no painted spaces since the area was not paved, but folks managed to keep their vehicles in fairly straight, orderly rows just the same.

He was moving so fast he almost passed the small figure huddled next to the rear tire of a full-size truck.

"Emma?"

Travis's heart had already been pounding. When she didn't move at the sound of his voice it felt as if it was about to beat its way out of his chest. "Emma!"

He dropped to his knees at her side. "Are you hurt?"

Still, she didn't respond. Not even when he gently touched her shoulder. Her head was bowed, her hands pressed tightly over her face. The only discernible movement was the trembling that shook her whole body.

Grasping her shoulders, Travis gently helped her stand, continuing to provide support when he sensed how unsteady she was.

With a finger under her chin he lifted her face and looked into her eyes. They were open yet devoid of emotion.

Pulling her into a tight embrace, he faced the men who were hurrying to his side.

"Call an ambulance," Travis ordered, further shaken by the powerless inflection of his own voice.

He had promised to keep Emma safe and had failed. Now, he wondered if this incident had sent her back into the labyrinth of her confused, battered mind.

If it had, he wasn't sure she'd ever emerge again.

White ceiling. Faded greenish walls. Dim light. A scream formed in Emma's throat, then died there.

Her eyelids fluttered for a moment before opening all the way. This place was far too clean and antiseptic smelling to be the dingy room where she'd been confined for endless days and nights. So where was she? And why?

The scene in the church parking lot returned in full detail—except for the aftermath of the shooting.

"Travis!"

Someone took her hand. "I'm here, Emma."

She could hardly believe her senses. The weary face looking down at her and trying to smile was him, all right, except he looked as if he'd been having a really rough day.

Gently, cautiously, he stroked her cheek with his free hand. "Welcome back, honey."

"Back? Back where?"

"You're in a hospital."

"Why? What am I doing here?"

"How much do you remember."

"We were at church. I sang a song and…" She inhaled deeply. "Then I saw Jet start down the center aisle and I made a run for it."

"Who?"

"The big guy. The bass player. His nickname is Jet. I remembered that much just before I saw him take a shot at you." Her gaze traveled over him quickly. "Are you okay?"

"Yes. He missed me."

"Did you shoot him?"

"No. Unfortunately, I missed, too."

"Then what happened to him?" She leaned slightly to the side so she could see the rest of the hospital room and the open door. "If he got away…"

"Harlan's joined forces with the Serenity police department and they're making a coordinated search. They'll get him."

"I wish I believed that." Slumping back against the pillows, she squeezed her eyes shut so tightly they began to hurt.

"I'll call the sheriff in a minute and relay the name you remembered. It might help narrow the search."

"I thought so, too, until I realized it's not the guy's real name."

"That doesn't mean there's no record of him using an alias," Travis reminded her. "Every clue helps."

"What about Sissy? Has the sheriff come up with any information about her?"

"Only that Blake has legal custody now that his wife is in prison. Maybe that's why you were with him in the first place. For the child's sake. I can see you sacrificing your own well-being to keep your promise to look after her."

Emma already felt as if a thousand unruly elves with ball-peen hammers were trying to pound their way out of her skull. She pressed her fingertips to her temples and tried to concentrate through the throbbing pain.

"I think that's how it all started," she said with a scowl. "But that's not why he locked me up later."

"Are you sure?"

"No," she said, disgusted. "But it seems right."

"Okay. I'm not supposed to use my cell phone in here so I'll just step outside and fill Harlan or Adelaide in on the new things you remembered."

Emma reached to give his warm hand a parting squeeze. He looked back at her, smiling yet sad looking at the same time. His dark eyes gleamed as if his emotions lay very close to the surface.

She held on long enough to ask, "What's wrong? Are you keeping something from me?"

"No." He was shaking his head and gazing at her as if seeing her for the first time in aeons.

"Then why do you look upset?"

"When I found you, hiding in the church parking lot, you were acting even more confused than when you first came home. I was afraid I'd lost you for good."

She made no comment as he turned to walk away and made a covert swipe at his cheek to cover his loss of self-control. Only someone who truly cared for her, who had forgiven her, would be that moved about her tenuous state of mind. *Dear Travis*. What a special man. What a special friend.

She was certain it was seeing him become the target of Jet's bullets that had nearly destroyed her this time. Thankfully, despite the recent trauma, she was continuing to heal, to regain her former self. And that meant it was only a matter of time before she was able to recall the entire story and give law enforcement the details they needed to find and rescue Sissy.

Perhaps, in the process, she'd also be able to free the child's mother by testifying against Blake and the others, Emma mused.

She closed her eyes and said a brief prayer, asking for that very outcome.

As soon as Travis returned she intended to ask him to take her home again. Now that she was lucid and functional, there was no reason to stay in the hospital.

Besides, she felt like a sitting duck lying in that bed. Everybody and his uncle probably knew exactly where she'd been taken and why. Word would surely reach Blake and the others. As long as she remained this exposed to outsiders, there was a good chance he'd make another attempt to frighten the secret out of her.

Emma heaved a sigh of frustration. "I wish I knew what I'm supposed to be hiding. At least that way I'd be able to judge whether or not it's important enough to risk my life for."

It must be, or she'd have told him everything when he was holding her prisoner, she reasoned. Which was all the more reason to keep dodging him until she did remember. Whatever truth was floating around in the deepest reaches of her subconscious, it would eventually surface. And when it did she was going straight to the sheriff.

A thin nurse wearing green scrubs and a matching hat that tied in the back entered the room. Head down, she was maneuvering a wheelchair closer to Emma's bed. That was a good sign. Maybe Travis had arranged for her release while he'd been out of the room.

Sitting up, Emma smiled. "Wonderful. No offense, but I can hardly wait to get out of here."

The nurse left the chair by the bed and returned to close the door before saying, "Get dressed."

"Gladly."

She found her clothing in a neat pile in a plastic bin below the nightstand and dumped the articles onto the bed, then hurriedly donned them.

"Be sure to thank whoever it was who folded this skirt for me," Emma said. "It's borrowed and I'd hate to have to return it all wrinkled."

"That's the least of your worries right now," the nurse said.

Something in her tone gave Emma pause. She froze. Stared. Saw the green-clad figure turn and smile.

It wasn't a real nurse—nor was it a woman. Blake's

skinny, pimply, younger brother, Ben, had apparently stolen the outfit and had passed through the hospital corridors unquestioned.

Emma's quick side-to-side glance caused him to laugh.

"Forget tryin' to run off. Blake and Jet are here, too, watchin' the exits in case you give me the slip. You won't get away this time."

At that moment, Emma's biggest concern was not for her own safety. She was worried Travis would return and be hurt. At this close range, surely no shooter would miss.

A tentative knock on the door to the hospital room caused both Emma and her adversary to jump. Instead of Travis's voice, however, they heard that of a woman gaily sing out, "Candy striper. I have a flower delivery for Ms. Landers."

"Don't let her in," Emma begged, hoping to protect another innocent person.

"Have to or they'll get suspicious and we'll never get out of here," Ben said flatly. He had a hand in his pocket, indicating the presence of a gun, as he unlocked the door and stepped aside.

The flowers were nearly as big as the woman who bore them. They were arranged in a deep ceramic dish, the blossoms spreading past her shoulders and masking most of her face. When she strolled through the door and asked, "Where do you want them, dear?" Emma was so shocked she nearly gasped.

"Um. I don't know," she managed to squeak.

Ben had remained in the background, almost hidden behind the door. That position also put him right next to the bathroom.

"Tell you what, suppose I just duck in here and add a bit of fresh water so they don't wilt?"

Before anyone could stop her, the woman with the bouquet headed straight for the bathroom. When she got close to where Ben was standing, she said, "Excuse me, dear. I just need a sec to see to these posies."

Emma watched, holding her breath, as Ben turned slightly and stepped out from behind the door. Because he intentionally kept his face averted, he provided the perfect target.

The heavy ceramic container rose in the air behind him as its bearer brought it down on the back of his head.

Emma lunged for him as he fell, closing her hand on his wrist in case he was conscious enough to fire the gun hidden in his pocket. She needn't have worried. He collapsed like a marionette without strings.

"There," Cleo said, dusting off her hands as if ridding herself of the rubbish under the flowers on the floor. "One down. How many more to go?"

"At least two," Emma said. "Give me a hand."

Grabbing the slightly built guitarist under the arms, she started to drag his limp body while Cleo lifted his legs by the ankles.

"Where are we going to put him?" the older woman asked.

"On the bed. I can tape him to the rails," Emma said. "While I'm doing that, you take his gun out of his pocket and aim it at him just in case."

"My pleasure." Cleo was grinning from ear to ear. "I've never conked anybody like that before so I wasn't positive it would work."

"How did you even know he was in here?"

"I saw him in the hall, dodging a local newspaper reporter who was trying to get in to see you. I thought he looked awful ugly for a nurse. That's when I realized I knew him from when he was a kid."

"What happened to Travis? I hope he's okay."

"He's fine. Last I saw, he was talking to that cute deputy, Adelaide Crowe."

Emma knew she was being baited so she schooled her features before answering. "Then he's safe."

"From this bunch of no-goods," Cleo drawled. "How safe he may be from a pretty woman is another question."

"Travis and I can never go back and take up where we left off, so you might as well stop trying to make me jealous," Emma said. She busied herself pulling off lengths of adhesive tape and wrapping Ben's wrists to the bed rails.

"Okay," the older woman replied. "Don't say I didn't warn you."

THIRTEEN

By the time Harlan had decided that the others had escaped and had been assured that Ben was well enough to be hauled off to jail, Travis was on his way home with Emma.

Cleo had left the hospital, too, detouring through town to apologize to the passengers she'd left stranded at church that morning when she'd hopped in her car and followed the ambulance carrying Emma.

"You should have seen your aunt in action," Emma told Travis, her grin wide, her eyes sparkling. "It was like a scene in a slapstick comedy. In she came, acting all innocent, and then *wham,* she bashed Ben so hard he never knew what hit him."

"Good thing she didn't do any permanent damage," Travis countered. He chuckled quietly as he pictured his aunt going on the offensive. "I wouldn't want to see Cleo spending time in the slammer for assault with a deadly daisy."

Emma laughed, then sobered. "Speaking of jail, I think it may be time for me to bite the bullet and let Harlan arrange for me to visit Robbie."

"You sure?"

She shrugged. "No. But I can't see any other options, can you?"

"Well, you could wait to remember more. Until the incident this morning you were really making progress."

"I still am," she insisted. "I did remember Jet's name."

"Under duress, too," he said, continuing to smile. "You're remarkable."

"Thanks. I'd settle for having half a mind."

"You're just a bit rattled right now. You'll get over it. I know you will."

"How can you be so sure?"

Travis took a deep breath while choosing his words carefully. "Because I heard you sing this morning." Taking his eyes off the road for an instant, he glanced over at her before adding, "I've never heard you sound more beautiful or put so much emotion into any song. It was amazing, Emma. Truly amazing."

Assuming she'd express doubt or modesty, he was surprised when she nodded and agreed with him.

"Something special happened to me this morning. I don't understand it but I think maybe God was blessing me for coming home. All during that hymn I felt as if I was singing just for Him."

"It showed."

"Good."

"I was wrong," Travis said with a slow nod.

"About what?"

"You. Your music. Asking you to stay in Serenity when you have so much talent was selfish. I should have either let you leave with my blessing or gone with you to Nashville."

"I wish you had," Emma said quietly. "But it's too late. We can't go back."

"We might be able to start over," he suggested, holding his breath as he waited for her reply.

It didn't come. Emma simply eased back in the truck seat and began to gaze out the window at the passing scenery, making her negative opinion as clear as if she'd stated it openly.

Emma was unwilling to try again with him, not that he blamed her. She'd found a different life in the city and had enjoyed the accolades of fans, just as she had that morning in church. Her talent was real. Incredible. And should be shared with the world.

Travis huffed. In taking her to church with him he had hoped she would see that Serenity was where she truly belonged. Instead, the opposite had happened. Because he had been given a glimpse of Emma's special gift that had blown him away, he could no longer deny that he'd been wrong all along. She was wasting her amazing ability by staying in the little Ozark town and he was not going to try to stop her when the time came for her to leave again.

Even if it broke his heart to release her and wish her well in her new life, he was going to advise her to follow her dreams. It was the only fair thing to do.

Travis's jaw clenched. He could do it. He would do it. No matter what it took to convince Emma to take advantage of the opportunities the good Lord provided, he was going to stick to his decision.

For her sake.

And for the sake of all the folks who were going to be uplifted listening to her blessed voice.

An overwhelming sense of loss flowed over and through him. Letting Emma go after all this, when they'd faced danger together and had relied upon each other so dramatically, was going to be *much* harder than it had been before. And their previous goodbye had nearly destroyed him.

The sun had passed its zenith when Travis pulled into the long drive leading to his property. Emma squinted against the brightness and shaded her eyes with her hand while peering ahead.

"I think I see a car in your yard. Could Cleo have beat us home?"

"I doubt it. She'd want to tell her friends all about her adventure in the hospital. Knowing her, that won't be quick." Travis slowed and leaned on the steering wheel. "Besides, her car is blue. That one's silver."

"Maybe you'd better stop out in front and see who it is before driving around back."

"My thoughts exactly," he said.

"Thank goodness you have your gun with you."

"Um, not exactly. The city police confiscated it at church."

"Uh-oh. Not good."

Judging by the stern look he gave her in reply, Travis agreed. "You stay in the truck. This time, I mean it."

"You meant it before," Emma said with a smirk she couldn't subdue. She realized he was deathly serious, yet her impish side kept insisting the situation could not possibly be that dire. After all, it was a sunny Sunday afternoon, the police had Ben in custody and chances were good that when the patrol cars had surrounded both the church and the local hospital, Blake and Jet had made themselves scarce. They might be malicious but they weren't stupid.

Travis rolled his eyes. "Will you please try to be serious for once, Emma?"

"I'll try, but it's hard when I'm so thankful to be alive. What an incredible morning we had."

"I'd like to think the rest of the day will be more peaceful," Travis said flatly. He brought the truck to a full stop directly behind the late-model silver-gray sedan.

Fidgeting, Emma pointed. "Look. Tennessee plates."

"So, I see."

Emma's mood crashed. All desire to tease vanished. Her pulse hammered. Her breathing grew ragged. With trembling fingers she reached for the door handle.

"No!" Travis almost shouted. "Stay here."

She meant to do as he'd ordered. She really did. But when she looked past the strange car and saw movement in the shade of the covered front porch she couldn't stop herself.

A frail-looking little girl was standing alone on the top step. Her golden hair was messy, her clothing baggy and dingy, yet Emma knew instantly who it was.

She bailed out of the pickup truck. "Sissy!"

With open arms, the child met her at the foot of the stairs. "Emma!"

Both were weeping tears of joy as they embraced. The child's reedy voice rose. "Where did you go, Emma? Why did you leave me?"

She kissed Sissy's fine hair and smoothed it back so she could meet her querulous gaze. "I was sick, honey. I would never have left you otherwise. I didn't know what I was doing."

Until that moment, Emma had not noticed anyone else on the porch. When she heard Travis coming up behind her she was so overcome she just wanted to share the joy.

Lifting Sissy while the child's arms were wrapped around her neck, Emma blinked back tears and grinned as she turned to him. "This is Sissy."

From the porch came a drawl that was also very familiar. Blake Browning said, "We've missed you, too, Emma."

Survival instinct spurred her closer to Travis, including the child in their mutually protective embrace. The more Emma stared up at Blake, the more she recalled. Although her thoughts were still random rather than well organized, she was certain of a few salient points.

One, she feared this man above all others. Two, he was Sissy's father. Three, her friend Robbie had been terrified of crossing Blake.

Travis pushed Emma and the child behind him and stood firm. "Get out of here. You're not welcome."

"I can see that," the fair-haired man replied, grinning to expose badly stained teeth. "We'll go. I just thought Emma might like to see Sissy again. They used to be real good buddies."

"Let me take care of her for you," Emma pleaded. "You know I'll do a good job. I promised Robbie."

"So, you did." He'd sauntered down the steps and stopped barely five feet away. "I'd like to talk to you about that while I'm here." He eyed Travis. "In private."

Travis stayed between them and palmed his cell phone, keying 911 with his thumb. "No way," he said. "You can either get in your fancy car and leave now, or wait for the sheriff. It's up to you."

"Emma wants to talk to me, don't you?" Blake challenged, pinning her with his narrowing gaze.

She shook her head and held the child close. "I have nothing to say to you."

"If you care about Sissy you'd better reconsider," he warned, pointing down the driveway. "Step over there with me right now or, I swear, you'll never see the kid again."

By this time, Sissy was clinging so tightly to Emma's neck she could hardly breathe. At that very moment, when she had the child in her arms, Emma felt safe in resisting Blake. The fact that he was Sissy's father, however, gave him the upper hand legally, whether anybody liked it or not.

Turning to Travis, she reluctantly passed the clingy little girl to him and reassured them both. "I'll just be a second. You can stand here and watch. It'll be all right."

Her gaze captured Travis's as she untangled herself from Sissy's tight hold. Emma willed him to understand. To let her do this her way without interference.

"It'll be okay," she whispered, kissing the child's cheek. "Trust me. This is a very nice man. He's my friend, too."

One tentative step backward told her Travis was going to let her to talk to Blake alone. If they had not had the child to worry about, Emma doubted her protector would have been nearly so accommodating.

Blake Browning led the way, his walk the proud strut of a victor. Well, Emma mused, let him think he'd won if that was what it took to get him to leave her alone. Besides, the longer she managed to stall him, the more chance that the sheriff would arrive in time to take him into custody.

Lurking in the back of her mind was the suspicion that there was little or no evidence against Blake that would warrant his immediate arrest. Unless they could get Ben to talk, to reveal the names of everyone involved in the plot against her, Harlan wouldn't be able to hold Blake for very long even if he did run him in.

Trembling, Emma crossed her arms to help still her telltale nervousness and positioned herself so she could look back at Travis and Sissy as well as face her nemesis.

"Okay. Here I am. What is there to talk about?"

He cursed colorfully. "You can't fool me. You know what I want."

"Actually, I don't," Emma said flatly, amazed at how strong and settled she felt inside. "If you'd done your homework you'd know I have amnesia."

"Yeah, right." He snorted. "You recognized Sissy and me."

"I haven't forgotten everything. Just the worst times. Some of the things that happened to me are coming back, but until the other day I couldn't even remember Robbie's name."

"That's really too bad. For you and for the kid," he said, sneering to demonstrate disbelief. "I'm disappointed in you, Emma. I thought you were a lot smarter than my wife." He chuckled without mirth. "Maybe that's the problem. Maybe you're too smart for your own good."

"I don't know what you're talking about. I barely remember a thing about Robbie."

"I suppose you don't know why she confessed and landed in prison, either."

"No, I don't." Waiting, Emma silently prayed that his over-inflated ego would prod him to tell her more.

"Then listen up." Blake stepped closer and bent to speak, lessening any a chance of being overheard. "I told her she could either take the fall for the rest of us or I'd see that Sissy disappeared. For keeps. And I'm telling you the same thing. If you don't tell me where my thieving wife hid all that money she took from me and the boys, you won't ever see the kid again, either."

Thunderstruck, Emma stared at him. There was an element of truth behind his appalling claim and more than one way to interpret it. Robbie might have hidden something from the others if she'd thought doing so would protect her child, planning to use the missing loot as a tool to guarantee Sissy's safety. *That* was how Emma intended to play this.

"If anything happens to that little girl," she warned, hands fisted on her hips, "I will see to it that whatever money Robbie hid goes up in flames. I'll put a match to it myself."

"Nobody's that crazy."

"I am. Ask anybody. I was totally out of my head when you got through with me. If I hadn't escaped I'd probably have stayed so mixed up I'd never have recovered."

To her surprise, Blake began to laugh louder. "Yeah, well, that didn't go quite like I thought it would."

A tremor zinged up Emma's spine. "What do you mean?"

"Just what I said. How do you think you managed to

get away from me? Huh? I'd had you chained up tight, yet suddenly you were able to get loose. Doesn't that seem strange?"

"Maybe Sissy let me go."

"Oh, she did. Following my orders. What surprised all of us was that you took off without her. I'd figured you'd grab her and head for the money so you'd have something to live on while you tried to keep me from finding you. Unfortunately, you didn't behave the way I'd expected. That's why I had to track you down the hard way."

"You let me go?"

"Sure. I was beginning to think you'd be too panicked to find the key I'd put under the mat. When you finally did, you took off so fast I lost sight of you."

"But you knew I'd come here?"

"I had a hunch. After all, where else would you go?"

Where else, indeed, Emma thought, chagrined. She had led Blake and the others right to the one place where she'd felt safe—and had thereby spoiled it, as well.

"All right," Emma said, bluffing and praying she'd be able to fool him, at least until she could come up with a better plan. "I'll consider telling you what you want to know if you'll let me take care of Sissy."

"I might. I might not. You'll have to spill Robbie's secret before I make up my mind."

"Let me keep her tonight while I sleep on it. I'll give you my answer in the morning."

"And let you sic the law on me before then? No way, lady."

"I won't say a word. I promise."

Blake's eyebrows arched and he stared at her. "Better not. Either you keep your mouth shut or the deal's off, understand?"

"Yes." In the distance she thought she heard sirens. "Sounds to me as if you'd better get going or you'll meet

Harlan Allgood again whether you like it or not. You remember him, don't you?"

"Oh, yeah. He was a smart-aleck deputy when me and Ben were kids. Never could take a joke."

"This is no joke," Emma told him. "If you expect to stay ahead of the cops, you'd better leave your daughter with me now and get going." His hesitancy made her wish she had Cleo's shotgun at hand.

Blake shook his head. "No way. The kid's my insurance. And don't try anything funny. Remember what I told you."

"I remember."

Hurrying back to rejoin Travis, Emma kissed Sissy's cheek again and forced a smile. "I'll see you again soon," she told the child, holding out her arms. "Come on, honey. Time to go with your daddy."

Walking close beside her, Travis resisted handing over the clingy child. "You're not going to give her back to that, that…"

Emma could tell he was restraining himself rather than speak too plainly. "It's just for one night," she said with an exaggerated wink, praying he'd realize she was actually hoping to come up with a counterplan in spite of the way her actions appeared.

His head was cocked, his brow furrowed, as Travis reluctantly released the little girl to Emma so she could carry her to the car.

Satisfied, Blake slid behind the wheel. "Put her in the booster seat in the back and hurry it up. Those sirens are gettin' too close for comfort."

Opening the sedan's rear door on the side opposite the driver, Emma saw not only the child's safety seat but an assortment of stuffed toys, Sissy's jacket and a small, crumpled blanket.

Slowly, purposefully, Emma leaned in. She now knew

exactly what to do, but so much depended on close timing she wasn't certain her plan would succeed.

Instead of placing the girl where she belonged, Emma set her on the floor of the car and leaned across the booster seat to hide what she was really doing.

"I can't find the seat belt," she said, stalling and listening to the crescendo of more than one siren swell in the background. *Hooray!* Harlan had company.

She kept her head down and used her long hair and her shoulders to block Blake's view so he couldn't see her substitute a teddy bear for Sissy. Then she draped the child's jacket over the stuffed toy. A silly ruse like that wouldn't fool anybody for long but it was the only chance they had.

While she remained half in and half out of the car and continued to stall, Emma whispered to Sissy, "Slide out and hide behind me."

For a few chilling moments she wondered if Sissy was going to balk. Then, she slithered out.

A quick peek showed that not only had the child escaped, Travis had seen her do it and had gathered her up. She was safe. For the present, anyway.

Emma kept listening and fussing with the seat belt, pretending to be doing as she'd been instructed. She didn't dare give Blake time to realize that his daughter was not actually in the vehicle with him until the police were almost upon them.

"Forget the belt. I'm out of here," Blake barked, dropping the car into gear.

It lurched forward. Emma felt the edge of the door opening bang into her shoulder. "Wait!"

He didn't, of course. She'd been counting on that. With a mighty lunge, Emma threw herself backward. The car's forward momentum slammed the door.

Landing flat on her back on the edge of the driveway,

Emma watched Blake speed off. If he stopped and tried to return at this point, he'd meet the sheriff for sure.

What a man like that would do after being outsmarted was anybody's guess. Emma figured whatever form of retaliation he chose, it was not going to be pleasant.

She smiled through tears of joy and temporary pain. She'd saved Sissy. Now all she had to do was remember enough about her past to save herself.

FOURTEEN

Travis could barely believe his eyes. Not only had Emma risked her own life, she'd almost let Blake get away with Sissy.

Holding the child's hand, he was beside Emma in moments. "What in the...?"

With a grin that belied the hard landing he'd seen her make, Emma rolled onto her hands and knees before standing up. "Whew! That was close."

"Of all the idiotic..."

Emma had been brushing herself off. Now she raised a hand. "Simmer down. I knew what I was doing."

"I strongly doubt that."

"It worked, didn't it?"

Anger was only part of his problem and he knew it. When he'd seen Emma dive backward as the car roared away, he'd been so alarmed he didn't think his pulse was ever going to slow down.

If Harlan hadn't pulled up at that moment, he was afraid he'd have said something he'd have regretted.

"It was Blake Browning," Travis shouted in the open patrol-car window while Emma knelt and hugged the child. "He's driving a silver sedan with Tennessee plates. He went that way. You can still see his dust."

The sheriff grabbed his radio and began giving backup

officers instructions to intercept their quarry as he continued the pursuit.

Travis turned on his heel, scooped up Sissy without another word and headed for the house. He didn't have to look behind to know Emma was following. By looking after Sissy, he'd pretty much guaranteed that Emma would stick close.

"Are you hungry?" Travis asked, directing his question to the child in his arms.

Sissy shook her bowed head.

"You feel pretty hungry to me," he continued, taking care to speak softly and be very gentle. If Emma's trauma was any indication of what this poor kid had been through, she must be equally fragile. Perhaps more so, considering her young age and probable lack of background in a loving home environment.

Continuing into the kitchen, Travis smiled. "Let me see your finger?"

Tentative, yet apparently trusting him, Sissy displayed an index finger.

"Oh, yeah," he said, pretending to test it with a light touch. "That one's definitely empty. I imagine the others are, too. You need milk and cookies."

"Cookies?"

That was the first word the girl had spoken to him. His smile grew to a wide grin. "Yup. Homemade. Pretty soon you'll get to meet Cleo, the lady who baked them, but for right now how about you and Emma and I sit down at the table and do a taste test? I'll give you one of each kind and you can tell Aunt Cleo which is your favorite when she gets home."

"Hand washing comes first," Emma said. "Bring her over to the sink."

Although Travis did as she'd suggested, he also whispered to Sissy, "Is she always this bossy?"

The child's head bobbled. She might not be enough at ease to talk much, but thankfully her trembling had stopped.

While Travis held her over the sink, Emma helped her suds and rinse her hands, then she wet the corner of a paper towel and wiped her face. "There. That's much better."

He carried Sissy to the table and put her in a chair before pulling a milk carton out of the refrigerator and giving it a shake. "We're going to need more of this if our house guest stays long," he said, raising an eyebrow at Emma.

"I suspect she'll be taken by Social Services as soon as we tell them her story," Emma said aside, hoping the child couldn't hear. "Unless you have some objection, I'd like to wait awhile before we report exactly what's happened."

"Suits me. Where will she sleep?"

"With me. And Bo." Emma smiled across the table at Travis, then explained to the girl, "Bo is a wonderful dog who keeps me company sometimes. He's very smart."

Sissy cupped a hand around her mouth and leaned closer to whisper to Emma.

"No. He doesn't bite like the mean dogs your daddy used to have," Emma said. She looked to Travis and he saw her brow knit. "I remember a little about them. They were chained to trees around the place where I was locked up. I was never afraid of them, but I always worried about Sissy getting too close and maybe getting hurt, so I warned her to keep her distance."

"That's a good idea," Travis agreed. "You should never trust any animal unless you're already friends or its owner is there to introduce you."

He noticed that Emma had sobered as she poured the child's milk. "I want to keep Bo with me—with us—as long as Sissy is here. That way nobody can sneak up on us."

"Fine. I also think it would be wise to contact Samantha Rochard-Waltham again."

"Why? Am I sounding more confused?"

"Not at all." Travis placed a well-worn, red-patterned tin on the table and lifted its lid to display three different kinds of homemade cookies. "Samantha volunteers for CASA."

"What's that?"

"Court Appointed Special Advocates for children," he explained. "A judge will assign one CASA worker per child and that person will speak for abused or abandoned kids who can't or won't defend themselves. Sissy is a prime candidate for assistance like that."

"Not if it means I won't be able to keep her with me. I promised her mother. Blake has no right to her."

"In your eyes, maybe not. In the eyes of the law, however, he's probably the only one who does have parental rights. Robbie's still in jail, isn't she?"

He glanced at the child to see if he'd misspoken and found her undisturbed by the mention of prison.

Emma was nodding and making a face. "I'd rather walk barefoot on burning coals than let her go back to him."

"That probably won't be necessary," Travis said. "Particularly if Harlan gets his hands on the guy and his Neanderthal partner pretty soon." He paused to smile at Sissy and hold up another cookie. "Good, huh?"

She nodded so vigorously she dropped crumbs all over the napkin she'd been using as a makeshift plate.

"Do you want me to phone Samantha for advice while you two finish your snack?" Travis asked.

"I guess you should. Only don't tell her too much. I want a little more time to remember exactly how I got into this fix in the first place."

"Meaning?"

Travis could tell by Emma's expression that she was wrestling with the decision of whether or not to explain, so he waited. And prayed.

Finally, Emma said, "It's something Blake reminded

me of when I was talking to him today. He insists Robbie told me an important secret." She hesitated and eyed the child, then went on. "I'm supposed to know where she hid some money. Apparently a lot of it. And I have absolutely no idea what he's talking about. At least not yet."

"None?"

"None. Nada. Zilch," Emma said with a grimace. "I don't have a clue what Robbie did or didn't tell me. I can barely remember her face, let alone confidences she may have shared."

"Mama's real pretty," Sissy told her softly. "Pretty like you."

All Travis could think to say at that moment was, "Amen," and he figured it was far wiser to keep his mouth shut. He could see how attached Emma was to Sissy and vice versa. The problem was the legality of their relationship. Emma was already in plenty of trouble without running afoul of the law over custody of the child. There had to be a way to protect them both.

The way he saw it, his best choice was to level with Samantha and let her take it from there. She was not only fair, she was acquainted with the rules governing mistreated children. If anybody could figure a way out of this, it was a pro like her.

And in the meantime? In the meantime, he was going to either insist the cops give his gun back immediately or borrow a sidearm from a friend until they did.

Nobody, not a behemoth like Jet or a skunk like Blake, was going to get to Emma—or Sissy—without going through him, first. He'd never been around kids much but this one had gone straight to his heart.

Once, he had wondered if he'd be able to love a child that was Emma's and not his. Now, he realized it was possible to care deeply about anyone who needed him the way they both did. He would not fail them.

And, God willing, he'd see to it that they had a chance for the future happiness they deserved—with or without him.

Excusing himself from the table, he fisted his phone and stepped out the back door to make his call to Samantha. That's when he noticed unusual, double-wide tire tracks in the dirt between the house and barn. Tracks from a truck, not the silver sedan. These were just like the ones that had been at the scene of the ATV shooting a few nights before.

Travis reached back inside the house and picked up Cleo's shotgun. It looked as if someone had circled the house and although the dogs weren't acting upset at present, he wasn't willing to take chances.

He put away his phone, checked to make sure the .12 gauge was loaded, and headed straight for the barn.

Emma had caught Travis's eye as he'd closed the door behind him for the second time. It was a relief to see him return for the shotgun. There was no sense making himself an easy victim when he had a choice of self-defense. Some folks might not understand country ways, might even call them primitive, but she knew better. When a person was isolated in a rural environment, as they were, it was logical to employ whatever safety measures were necessary.

Sissy had picked up her glass with both hands and was drinking greedily.

"Take your time," Emma said gently. "There's plenty more where that came from. You don't have to hurry."

"Daddy bought me chocolate milk," Sissy said.

"Really?" Trying to hide her surprise, Emma smiled. "That's nice."

"He said I can have a puppy, too."

"Did he?"

"Uh-huh. After Mommy comes home."

The thought of poor Robbie languishing in jail sank

Emma's spirits like a rowboat with a gaping hole hacked in its bottom.

"I wish I could help her do that," Emma said.

"You can help Daddy," Sissy told her, pausing to stuff more cookie crumbs into her mouth before grabbing the milk again.

"I can?"

The slim five-year-old nodded vigorously. "Uh-huh. He said."

Feigning a casual reply, Emma leaned an elbow on the table and rested the side of her head in her hand. "Really? That's great. What else did your daddy tell you?"

"That he misses Mommy. He wants us to go on a vacation with her."

"Sounds like fun. What did he say I should do to help your mama?"

"Tell him where the treasure is."

"I see. Anything else?

Sissy's head bobbed, her tangled curls bouncing in a familiar way that reminded Emma of all the times when she'd worked so gently to pull a comb through the fine, golden strands.

That clear memory was a revelation. She *had* voluntarily looked after this child. And, for a while, had had no trouble getting along with Blake or the others—as long as they kept their distance.

It was only after Robbie had confided in her why she intended to confess to everything and throw herself on the mercy of the court that Emma's reactions to the men had changed. She knew the truth! Robbie was innocent and had been threatened, exactly the way Blake had insinuated.

She was also positive that Blake and the others had started out as honest musicians and had not turned to crime until their previous efforts to find success had failed miserably and they'd ended up deep in debt to questionable sources.

One of the most unexpected memories was how happy Blake and Robbie had once been and how they had both loved their daughter. How was it possible for any father to be a doting parent in the beginning, then a few years later use his child as a pawn in a criminal conspiracy?

A picture of his bad teeth popped into her mind and provided an answer. He'd become addicted, probably to meth. It was those desperate urges for more and more drugs that now drove him. That, and probably his outstanding debts; debts he could settle once he got his hands on the cache of stolen money he claimed Robbie had hidden.

Everything was starting to make sense, Emma mused, wishing Travis was present so she could tell him how she was finally putting the clues together.

Then again, she mused, smiling at Sissy, if Travis had stayed with them, the child might not have been relaxed enough to speak so openly.

In retrospect, Emma suspected the little girl had been well coached. And, given that conclusion, perhaps she had not been as clever as she'd thought when she'd smuggled Sissy out of Blake's car. If he had planned to use his daughter as his spokesperson, perhaps he had intended for her to stay behind all along.

The question then became how much more had Sissy been told to do and where did her true allegiance lie? Yes, she was only five years old. But she was smart as a whip and had been under her father's wing for longer than Emma liked to consider. Of course she wanted her mother back. It also stood to reason that she loved her father, no matter how abusive he may have been.

Emma cast a loving gaze at the needy child and vowed to help her out of the predicament her father's perfidy had created. It was not going to be easy. And it was likely that Sissy would misunderstand and end up hating her for what she had to do.

That couldn't be helped. Emma knew right from wrong, good from bad. Those traits were not open to interpretation as far as she was concerned.

She sighed, realizing one more thing. Keeping Sissy to herself was not in the girl's best interests no matter how much she would miss and worry about her once she was put into foster care. Travis was right. Again. They needed to involve the authorities and get professional help.

For Sissy's sake.

And, in the long run, for Robbie's, too.

Travis inspected the barn, found nothing amiss and made his call before returning to Emma. This time, he unloaded the shotgun before propping it in its familiar place.

"Good safety measure," Emma said. "You were gone a long time. What did Samantha say?"

"She's going to get in touch with a social worker, Brenda Connors, who will contact us at this number and make sure everything is legal." He held up his cell phone. "In the meantime, we're supposed to just carry on as we have been."

"For how long?"

Travis could tell Emma was dreading having to relinquish the child, yet he also realized she'd come to accept the inevitability of saying goodbye. "She didn't say. I asked her to take her time."

"Thank you."

"You're welcome." He lowered himself into a chair and propped his elbows on the table. "This has been quite a Sunday. I hope Cleo remembers she promised to pick up fried chicken at Hickory Station on the way home."

"Do they still make that? It used to be practically everybody's stop after church."

"Yup. Still do. It's a Southern institution."

"Fried chicken for Sunday dinner or getting it at that gas-station deli?"

Travis gave her a lazy smile. "Both." His gaze settled on Sissy. Her eyelids were drooping. "I think one of us is ready for a nap."

Emma nodded and reached over to gently rub the child's back through her oversize T-shirt. "Judging by the stuff that was crammed into Blake's car, she may have been sleeping there instead of in a bed. That would explain why she needs a bath and her clothes are dirty."

"Want me to carry her upstairs for you?"

"No. If she wakes and sees she's in a strange place she'll be frightened like I was when I first came here. Put her on the sofa and I'll keep her company."

Although he understood Emma's desire to stay near the girl, he couldn't envision her being satisfied to sit still and do nothing. "Want me to see if I can scare up a couple of Cleo's magazines so you'll have something to read?"

"No," Emma said, rising and making room so Travis could reach Sissy's chair. "Bring me the laptop."

"Have you remembered more?"

"Enough to do another internet search," she said. "I know Adelaide said we shouldn't look at other pictures until we'd seen the tapes from the store but we're sure the guy who grabbed me was Jet, and Ben's already in jail. That just leaves Blake, who may also be in custody by now, God willing. I want to look up that coffeehouse where the matchbook came from and see if it rings a bell."

He huffed. "I'd forgotten all about finding that. Sounds like your memory is working better than mine is right now."

What he didn't say was how his heart had nearly broken when he'd thought the accelerating car had injured her. Or how fervently he'd prayed when she'd fled from church, gone into shock and ended up in the hospital.

Easily lifting the small child and following Emma to the living room, he wanted to reach out to her, to pull her into a mutual embrace and hold them both closely, protectively, until all danger was past.

He wouldn't, of course. Emma wouldn't want him to show so much affection and it might also frighten Sissy, yet Travis could picture them as a family. A real family. One that trusted and relied upon one another the way he had been raised.

Poor kid. His heart went out to her as he gently placed her on the couch and saw her close her eyes almost immediately. He'd never pictured himself as a father before but it was getting easier by the minute. This little girl—and Emma—would make perfect additions to his life.

It was no more than a far-fetched dream, of course. Emma had shown little interest in renewing their romance and the child was bound to be placed in foster care after her father joined her mother in prison.

But…what if Blake got away again? Worse, suppose he escaped prosecution and conviction? What then?

The notion that Emma might never again be totally safe was so strong, so profound, he had to struggle to take a deep breath. To stand back. To turn away from her and leave the room the way his conscience insisted he must.

Every nerve in his body was screaming for him to return. To take Emma in his arms and hold her tight. To rain kisses on her hair the way he had when he'd helped her to her feet outside the church that very morning.

Only this time she'd realize he was kissing her. This time, if he was so foolish as to reveal his burgeoning feelings, he might scare her away for good.

In retrospect, he suspected that was exactly what he'd done when he'd proposed to her years ago. If he hadn't pressed her and insisted on commitment, maybe she wouldn't have panicked and run off with the band—and Blake Browning.

For the first time since Emma had been eighteen, Travis was able to stop blaming her for leaving. That should have given him peace but it didn't. Instead, it showed him how much of the blame was really his.

The trip to and from his office to deliver the laptop took only a minute or two.

His mental journey from past to present to future was far more problematic. No matter how much he hoped things would turn out otherwise, he could not see one good reason Emma would ever agree to forgive him and become his wife. Proposing again was likely to have the same result it had had before.

Besides, he reasoned, asking her to stop using her amazing singing voice was wrong. Her talent was God-given and should be shared with the world. Staying in Serenity, with him, would rob her of the professional career for which she was destined.

Travis's noble thoughts were immediately countered by his desire to tell Emma how he felt, to confess his love, even if she thought he was being silly and laughed at him.

He passed her the laptop and straightened, praying for guidance and waiting for the right moment to speak up.

Emma beat him to it. When she smiled at him and whispered, "Thanks. I don't know what I'd do if I didn't have a wonderful friend like you," he was rendered speechless.

Nodding and understanding far more than he wanted to, he turned on his heel and did the right thing. He walked away.

FIFTEEN

It didn't take Emma long to find the coffeehouse from the matchbook and pull up its website. There wasn't a lot to see beyond the usual shots of the cozy interior and one picture of the business logo that was an integral part of the facade. Because the café was located in a storefront on a Nashville side street, there wasn't much about it that was memorable. Seeing those pictures did, however, jog her memory.

There was somebody else she should remember. She knew there was as surely as she knew that the band's troubles had begun in the innocent-looking establishment she was studying on Travis's laptop. But who?

Emma knew it was a man whose face she needed to recall. Old? Young? Tall? Short? Nothing specific came to her other than the fact that he was somehow connected to the music business. Which meant he could be any one of the thousands of people she'd met in Tennessee—convincing strangers who purported to be talent scouts and were mostly out to line their own pockets at the expense of naive newcomers.

She did remember that happening to her group. They'd be promised a gig where some important record company executive was scheduled to be in the audience, then learn later that they'd been duped into performing for free.

Picturing fancy Stetsons and boots, she first thought of Blake's penchant for dressing like a drugstore cowboy. Then, she closed her eyes and saw more.

The man in this vision was tall and thin, with a luxurious mustache and graying hair. He always wore the finest suede jackets with long fringe and intricate, Indian beadwork across the yoke, front and back. His silver-toed boots were also unique, as was the rattlesnake's head and skin that made up his memorable hatband.

Since Sissy was sleeping so peacefully on the sofa, Emma decided to bide her time and wait for Travis's eventual return rather than call to him and chance waking the weary child.

The more she recalled, the harder it was to sit still. Although she didn't remember the man's name, she could imagine hearing his voice clearly.

"I'll make y'all famous," he'd drawled, flashing a smile that revealed a gold-capped tooth. "Shouldn't take long. All we need is a little luck and the right venues. Stick with me, boys—and girls—and you'll go places."

Emma suspected she had not liked him much to begin with, and that her opinion had not changed as time went on. He had manipulated Blake and the others until they'd run out of money, then had arranged for the loan that had sucked them deeper and deeper into debt.

"All we have to do is deliver packages of handbills to the guys who own some of the places where we have gigs," Blake had assured the others, "and we'll get bonuses."

Picturing that scene, Emma saw Ben and Jet laugh. She had glanced over at Robbie and seen her shrug as if missing the private joke. They both had. Until it was too late and they were entangled in a drug delivery system that had ultimately led to their downfall.

Emma concentrated and began to page through the in-

terior pictures of the coffeehouse a second time. There had
to be more clues here. Only there weren't.

Disgusted and more than a little frustrated, she left that
site and did a search for similar places in and around Nashville, noting the names of other small bands, then following up with searches for their promo.

That was where she hit the jackpot. All she could see
was the back of a fancy, Western-cut jacket but that was
enough. There he stood, applauding for another group of
musicians who were clearly playing their hearts out for
him and his cronies. How many others had there been?

A sound behind her made Emma jump. She whipped
her head around, then broke into a grin. "Travis! I'm so
glad you came back." She leaned aside and pointed to the
computer. "Look what I found."

"What? That's not Blake's band, is it?"

"No. Look at the guy next to the stage, the one with the
beaded jacket. I'm almost positive he's the one who got us
into so much trouble."

"You can't even see his face."

"I'd know that coat anywhere. I saw it often enough."

"Who is he?"

Her senses had shifted into high gear the moment Travis
had leaned over the back of the sofa to get a better view
of the screen. Nevertheless, her concentration was strong
enough to be certain when she replied, "I don't remember
his name. Not yet, anyway. But I'm sure he's the one who
promised Blake and the band so much and then involved
us in drug pushing. That has to be where it started."

"You're positive?"

"Not enough to testify under oath, if that's what you're
asking. I can't explain how I know, I just do."

"I believe you," Travis said, straightening and raking
his fingers through his hair. "So, now what?"

Emma cast a quick glance at the sleeping little girl. "I

feel like I need to take a short walk to help me think. Do you mind sitting here with Sissy for a few minutes?"

He made a face at her, bringing a smile back to Emma's expression and a lightness to her heart. "I'll behave," she said. "I promise. I just need a chance to pace. You should understand that. You've been doing the same thing."

"Only since you showed up," he countered, softening his remark with a smile of his own. "Okay. Hand me the laptop and I'll keep looking for that beaded jacket. Who does that guy think he is? He looks like he got caught in a time warp and belongs back in the fifties."

"A lot of people seemed to know him. He's not young. And I remember a thick, grayish mustache. If you happen to come across a picture of his face, holler."

"You'll be in the house, right?"

"Of course," Emma replied, briefly patting his shoulder as he carefully took her place at the end of the sofa. "I'm not planning to go anywhere else."

Noting the arch of Travis's eyebrows, she laughed softly and raised a hand, palm out. "I will *not* go outside. Scout's honor."

"You were never in scouting," he said, still staring as if trying to read her thoughts.

"No, but you sure impressed me when you got all the way up to Eagle Scout. I love a man in uniform."

The moment that revealing observation was out of her mouth she rued it. Truth to tell, she didn't have to see Travis Wright in a uniform to appreciate him. He looked wonderful in worn jeans or his Sunday best. It didn't matter. His welcoming smile and the sparks of emotion in his dark eyes were all it took to send shivers zinging through her and tear her wandering mind from anyone or anything else.

Which is detrimental, Emma mused soberly. Unless she pulled herself together soon and remembered everybody who had brought her grief, she and all her friends were going to remain in terrible jeopardy.

Deciding to change from the borrowed skirt so she could return it to Cleo, she headed upstairs to her room, noting as she stepped that a couple of risers squeaked and hoping that the noise hadn't awakened Sissy.

"Travis is right," she murmured, proceeding. "It all depends on me. I have to remember more."

Yet the harder she tried, the less clear her thoughts were. It was as if clouds had dropped from the sky to obscure the past like thick fog.

Surely the sun of recollection was still out there, bright and clear. All she had to do was wait for it to shine through and reveal everything.

That was the hard part. The waiting. The wondering. The sense of foreboding that kept insisting she was as guilty as the others had been and was simply refusing to admit it.

Crossing to the bedroom window, Emma looked out, leaned a shoulder against the sash and closed her eyes. "Father, I do want to know what happened. Really, I do. Even if it's bad."

Was that true? she asked herself, wondering what the penalty might be for lying to God.

"And if I'm fooling myself, please tell me that, too," Emma added to her prayer.

A distant noise caused her to open her eyes and squint down at the yard. Cleo's blue car was coming up the lane and leaving clouds of dust in its wake.

"We could use one of those spring showers, too, Father," she added. "The pastures need rain."

Spoken like a farmwife, Emma realized with a start that led to a wan smile. There had been a time...

"No," Emma insisted. "I don't belong here and I can't stay one second longer than I have to, for Travis's sake if not for my own. The more I start to imagine a future here, the worse it will hurt when I leave."

Talk about *truth!* Well, she'd asked for it, hadn't she? So what was she complaining about?

Slipping off the skirt and replacing it with a pair of jeans, she was about to put her tennis shoes on when she took another peek out the window.

Cleo's car was no longer visible but there was a lot of dust still hanging in the still air.

A shiver of awareness coursed through Emma, leaving her unsettled. Thinking something was wrong.

It was probably no more than a reaction of her already overstressed nerves to a normal sight and she was getting all worked up over nothing.

"No," she countered, spinning and starting back down the stairs barefoot. Nerves were the good Lord's early-warning system. Even if hers were overworked and misfiring, she was not about to ignore them.

Especially not now.

Travis heard Cleo arrive and call, "Come 'n get it before I feed it to the dogs!" just before the kitchen door slammed.

He decided food would do Sissy good. She was stirring, anyway, so he lightly tapped her foot. "Time to wake up and eat again," he said, taking care to keep his voice low and neutral.

That effort obviously wasn't enough. The child opened her eyes, sat up with a start and gave a tiny shriek.

Emma rounded the newel post at the bottom of the stairs and rushed to comfort her. "It's okay, honey. I'm here. You're safe."

Although the little girl had immediately wrapped her thin arms around Emma's neck, she was also peeking out at Travis. "I'm sorry I scared you, Sissy," he said. "The lady who bakes the cookies just came home with fried chicken and we need to go eat supper."

"I know you like chicken," Emma added.

Travis arched an eyebrow as if to ask if she truly did remember and was relieved to see her nod. Considering some of the medical case studies he'd read, Emma was making extraordinary progress. Part of that was undoubtedly due to being home in Serenity among friends, but he wasn't conceited enough to think that the Lord wasn't having a divine influence on her recovery, as well.

In this case particularly, Travis was more than willing to give God all the credit since he didn't seem to be able to help much. Other than to try to protect Emma and the child, he added, hoping his skills were sufficient and wondering if he ought to give Thad Pearson a call and ask for backup from the former military man. Maybe he would phone Pearson Products Monday morning when the factory opened and see if Thad would loan him a pistol, at the very least.

Cleo was bustling around the kitchen, setting out plates and silverware when the others joined her. She grinned. "Well, well, who's our guest?"

"This is my special friend, Sissy," Emma said. "Sissy, meet Aunt Cleo, the cookie lady."

"So this is Sissy. My, my, what a pretty little thing. Kinda reminds me of her grandma Browning. Without the wrinkles, of course." She chuckled to herself. "I bought the full dinner bucket. Figured I owed it to y'all since it took me so long to get home."

"We ate cookies while we waited," Travis said, smiling at the sleepy child. "Didn't we, Sissy?"

"Probably spoiled your supper and hers, too," his aunt said. "Oh, well, more for me and Emma."

"Emma had cookies, too," Sissy piped up.

That made Cleo laugh. "Oh, she did, did she? Well, well. I guess we won't need all these plates after all."

"Yes, we will," Travis said, helping her unload the bags and place the hot food in the middle of the table. "I'm starving."

"Okay, then grab a couple of phone books to raise that poor child up enough to see what's on her plate," Cleo ordered. "These chairs sit way too low for such a little thing."

"Yes, ma'am." It amused Travis to hear Cleo so animated and acting so in charge. "You must have had quite a time with all your friends this afternoon."

"Did I ever!" She joined the others around the table and bowed her head briefly to say a blessing on the food before digging in. "You should have heard Velma and Kate when I told them about knocking out that fella with a flowerpot."

"His brother Blake was here," Travis informed her. "That's how we got Sissy."

"Mercy. I thought I was the only one having an exciting day."

An unexpected knock at the front door made everyone pause to listen.

Emma was the first to speak. "I thought I saw more dust on the road after Cleo's car passed and I meant to mention it, but by the time I got downstairs I'd forgotten."

"Perfectly natural," Cleo said. "I do that all the time. Always have. If it wasn't real common, nobody would need a shopping list or one of those smarty-pants phones."

"Smart phones," Travis said, giving her a lopsided smile as he got to his feet. "I'll go see who's here." His gaze met Emma's and he quietly added, "It's probably Samantha Rochard-Waltham."

As he left the table he heard Emma add, "And the social worker."

"You called them?" Cleo asked, frowning.

"Travis did. I know it was for the best, I'm just having trouble thinking about letting Sissy out of my sight."

Listening, Travis had to agree. Parting was going to be hard on all of the adults, but his biggest concern was the child. If there was anything he could have done to change things for Sissy he would have. In a heartbeat.

His hand closed on the knob. He opened the door.

It wasn't Samantha and her friend as they had all supposed. It was Blake Browning. And he was armed!

Emma almost choked on a mouthful of food when she saw Travis reenter the kitchen and realized who was with him.

"Daddy!" the child squealed, clearly delighted. "We're having chicken."

"Sorry I can't stay for supper," Blake said. He extended his free hand toward his daughter. "Come on, Sissy. Time to go."

More tense than she'd ever imagined possible, Emma gripped the edge of the table. With Blake's gun trained on Travis's back, there was no way she was going to make a false move. Not when his life depended upon her keeping her cool.

"I—I haven't had time to remember much more," Emma said, stalling. "I've tried, but…"

Blake looked to his child for confirmation. "Is that true?"

Sissy nodded vigorously.

"Too bad," he said with a sigh. "I'd hoped having her with you would convince you to cooperate. Since you haven't, we'll try something else."

"Wait!" Emma was on her feet. "I did see a picture on the internet. It was our band's promoter, I think. Tall guy. Fringed jacket and silver-toed boots?"

Blake snorted derisively. "Yeah. That'd be good old Mack McLauchlin. He helped us, all right. Boy, did he."

"There were drugs involved, weren't there?" Emma pressed. "We delivered them."

"I thought you had amnesia," the armed man said with a sneer.

"I did. I do. Snatches of memory come to me and I have to try to make sense of them. Sometimes it works, sometimes it doesn't." She stepped in front of the child. "Please, don't take Sissy."

"And why shouldn't I?"

The little girl had been stuffing chicken in her mouth so her words were somewhat garbled. Unfortunately, they were clear enough for everyone to understand when she said, "We're waiting for a lady."

Blake's eyes narrowed, giving Emma the chills all the way to her core as he asked, "What lady? Were you dumb enough to call the cops again?"

"No." She raised her hand as if taking an oath. "I didn't tell the sheriff about Sissy."

"Then who's this lady you're expecting? What does she have to do with me?"

"Nothing," Emma snapped, realizing she may have spoken too quickly, sounded too anxious.

"Uh-huh. I'll bet." Browning once again held out his hand. "Come on, Sis. We're getting out of here."

In the background, Emma noticed Cleo sliding out of her chair and feigning nonchalance when she had to be feeling every bit as nervous as everyone else.

"You. Old woman. Sit."

"Old woman, my aunt Fanny," Cleo grumbled at him. "Keep your shirt on. I was just gettin' a container so I could send some of this food with you."

"I don't need your handouts."

"Maybe you don't but your little girl does. I'll fix her up a bag of cookies, too."

Emma's heart felt lodged in her throat. She knew where

the plastic bags were kept in the Wright kitchen and they were nowhere near where Cleo was headed.

The shotgun! Emma was at a loss. Cleo thought it was still loaded. If she picked it up and tried to use it, Blake would surely shoot her. At this close range, he couldn't miss.

She caught Travis's eye and thought she saw a slight nod. When he reached into his pocket and surreptitiously pulled out the shells he'd removed from the .12 gauge earlier, she was positive he understood.

"Cleo," Emma called urgently.

"Just a second."

"No." This time Emma shouted.

The older woman looked back. Followed Emma's gaze. Saw the red-colored cylindrical shells displayed in Travis's palm.

In the few moments it had taken for Cleo to come to her senses, Blake had grabbed his daughter's hand and was leading her away, apparently oblivious to the tableau taking place practically under his nose.

Emma and the others could do nothing but watch Sissy go and pray that Jesus would watch over her. Wherever her father took her. Whatever he decided to do next.

SIXTEEN

Travis kept his arms wrapped tightly around Emma to stop her from trying to follow Blake. She fought him, as he'd expected.

"Let me go!"

"No. You can't help Sissy by getting yourself shot. Calm down. Think. There must be something sensible we can do."

There were tears in Emma's eyes when she looked up at him. "What? You tell me and I'll gladly do it." Still struggling, she added, "Otherwise, let me go."

Instead, he pulled her closer. Every fiber of his being was screaming for him to go after Blake and the child, while the saner side of his brain insisted it could be literal suicide.

In the background, Travis heard his aunt phoning the emergency number shared by the sheriff, police and fire departments. As she explained the situation and reported that the child and her father were no longer on scene, he could tell by her responses that she was not happy.

"What's that got to do with it?" Cleo demanded. "Just go get him." Silent for a few moments, she blurted, "Oh, for cryin' out loud," and hung up.

Still holding tight to Emma, Travis looked over at the older woman. "What did they say?"

"That they're already lookin' for Blake and his partner. Knowing Sissy's with him will probably mean they won't chase his car. If they do spot him, they'll hang back and wait till he's alone."

By this time, Emma's struggles had eased enough that Travis loosened his grip, although he still kept her close. There was no way he'd let go completely and take the chance she'd somehow follow Browning.

The kiss he placed on her forehead when she turned her head and raised reddened eyes to him was so instinctive, so natural, he'd acted before he could stop himself.

If there was any special recognition in Emma's expression he missed it, considering himself fortunate that she either hadn't noticed or was willing to overlook the telling, emotional slip.

He was about to suggest that Cleo phone Samantha and advise her to cancel their visit when a car pulled up in the yard and stopped.

Emma twisted from his grasp and flew out the door, stopping on the porch.

Travis was right behind her. He realized immediately that these visitors were expected.

As Samantha and her companion climbed out of the white SUV, Emma sagged against a porch post.

Gently, relieved to feel little resistance, Travis stepped up and took the place of the post, pulling Emma back into his arms and holding her firmly, lovingly.

Maybe these women could advise them how to best rescue the little girl, he reasoned. Parental rights were strong, as they should be. Would it be enough that Emma had had an inside look at Browning's life and had judged it lacking? Likely even a danger to his daughter?

Although Travis's heart was breaking for Sissy, he was a realist. It was Jet and Ben who had been identified as Emma's actual assailants. As long as she was still befuddled about Blake's part in her abduction and imprisonment in Tennessee, there was no way the authorities were going to take her word for it. Their only real hope, at this point, was that Ben would implicate his brother and give Harlan a better reason to hold him once he was apprehended. If he ever was.

That notion settled in Travis's heart and sent chills down his spine. It was not enough to dislike and distrust Blake Browning. They needed positive proof of his criminal activities or he'd likely go free.

Emma needed to remember everything.

That was their only real hope of saving Sissy.

The arrival of Samantha Rochard-Waltham and Brenda Connors was anticlimactic to say the least.

Emma greeted Samantha politely before meeting the older, pleasantly plump, gray-haired social worker.

Brenda's twinkling eyes were framed by glasses that made them seem larger than life. Her relaxed manner and friendly smile were not enough to put Emma at ease, although she did manage to refrain from stating her case until introductions were complete.

"Why don't we all go inside?" Samantha suggested.

Emma noticed that both women were looking at Travis as if expecting him to explain further, but she jumped right in with her own version of the story.

"Sissy isn't here anymore," she said, struggling to keep from sounding as if she were barely holding back hysteria. "Her father came and got her just a few minutes ago."

Samantha patted Emma's arm. "I'm sorry to hear that. Have you remembered more about him?"

"He delivered drugs. He admitted it in front of all of us," Emma said, indicating Travis and Cleo.

"What about the child?" Brenda asked. "Was she well? Were there any signs of physical abuse?"

"Only that she was dirty, hungry and tired," Emma said. Her voice caught. "He threatened to make her disappear if I didn't help him find some money his wife hid."

"That doesn't necessarily mean he was going to harm her," Brenda offered. "He may have meant both of them were going into hiding."

"What if he didn't? What if he means to…" Emma could not put her worst fears into words.

"I'll list everything you said in my report," the social worker promised. "Why don't we go have a cup of coffee and you can tell me the rest?"

"We don't have time for coffee. We have to *do* something!"

"Legally," Samantha reminded her. "That's the way to win against a person like Sissy's father. If you don't jump through the right hoops you can make matters much worse."

"How could they possibly get worse than they are already?" Emma asked. Nevertheless, she led the way into the kitchen.

"There's plenty of extra chicken and fixin's, if you ladies are hungry," Cleo said, pouring two more mugs of hot coffee and serving their guests.

"Thanks. Maybe later." Brenda took a seat at the far end of the table and rearranged dishes to make room for her briefcase. "First, I need to get a few facts down on paper."

Emma was more than ready. She leaned forward, hands gripping the edge of the table, and waited, eager to proceed, to make some kind of progress no matter how simplistic and futile it seemed.

"Your name?"

"Emma Lynn Landers."

"Can you show me an ID? A driver's license will do."

"I—I don't have anything like that." She looked to Samantha for support. "Didn't you tell her what happened to me?"

"No. That was privileged medical information. You can fill her in right now if you want."

"Later," Emma said firmly. "The important thing is getting the proper authorities looking for Sissy. If you're right about Blake planning to disappear, every minute counts."

The social worker's gray head was nodding. "Absolutely. Now, what is the child's home address? Start with the county where she currently resides."

Flabbergasted, Emma could only stare. "What difference does that make?"

"Jurisdiction," Brenda replied. "Shall I put down Fulton County?"

"You'd better go back to the beginning and tell her everything," Travis interjected. "I have a feeling this meeting is not going to end quite the way we'd hoped."

Emma's spirits plummeted. He was right. She'd never considered that the more Blake and Sissy moved around, the harder it would be for any branch of the law to catch up to them. If they claimed to still have a home in Tennessee, there was probably little the authorities in Arkansas could do—unless he was caught committing another crime here.

As she began her convoluted tale of kidnapping, escape and memory loss, Emma was already making plans.

If she couldn't remember enough to nail him for prior crimes in Tennessee, she'd see to it that he broke the law in Arkansas.

First, she'd have to find a way to get word to him that she had regained her lost memory. Then, when he came for her, she'd let him think he had the upper hand before springing her trap.

It would have to include backup from the sheriff, she reasoned, but she'd keep her circle of confidants as small as possible, perhaps starting by informing the determined reporter who'd kept pestering her for an interview.

Above all, Emma told herself, she must not let Travis know. He'd surely try to stop her if he had any idea what she was up to—or even attempt to take her place.

She knew she was the only one who could pull this off. All she had to do was figure out how to adjust the jaws of her trap without having it snap shut before she was ready.

Night was encroaching by the time the nurse-practitioner and social worker left the Wright home. Travis had excused himself to take care of evening chores while the women told one another goodbye.

He could tell how upset Emma was to learn that her chances of successful intercession on behalf of Sissy were severely limited. And he sympathized. He simply didn't see what else they could do, short of breaking the law themselves and somehow stealing the child back from her father.

"Meaning, we'd go to jail and Blake would still win," Travis muttered to himself.

Therefore, their only real hope was for Emma to recall enough to warrant Browning's arrest for imprisoning her. If she couldn't even identify the place where she'd been locked up, how could they possibly convince anyone that the kidnapping had actually taken place?

When Travis came back inside with Bo, Emma was waiting for him. He glanced past her. "I take it they finally left?"

"Yes. What a waste of time."

"That's the disadvantage of being the good guys," he said. "We have to follow the law while the crooks can break all the rules they want."

She heaved a heavy sigh. "I'm beginning to see that a lot more clearly than I'd like."

It occurred to him to suggest they pray about it but he refrained from doing so. Emma's faith was probably stretched to its limits. His certainly was.

There was one other thing he had considered, yet he hated to even bring it up because it could cause her more anguish.

Folding her arms, she scowled at him. "Spill it."

"Spill what?"

"I don't know. But you have something on your mind. I can see the wheels in your brain spinning."

"You can, huh?"

"Yes. There are times when I can almost read your mind."

"That's scary."

"You have no idea." She managed a slight smile. "Might as well tell me. You know I never give up."

"True." He cleared his throat and stuffed his hands in his jeans pockets. "I was just wondering if you might want to try taking one of those sedatives again. They did help once."

Emma nodded soberly. "Yes. They did. I hadn't thought of that but you're right. I was probably going to lay awake half the night, worrying about Sissy, anyway."

"Okay, I'll tell Cleo to stand by."

When Emma gazed into his eyes and said, "It's you I want there if I panic again," Travis was momentarily taken aback.

"All right. I'll sit by you, too."

Her eyes misted and she sniffled, making him yearn to take her in his arms so strongly he nearly gave in. The memories of holding her close earlier in the day were so vivid he could almost feel her warmth, her trust, the way she'd leaned on him both literally and figuratively.

Yes, he would be there for her. Always. Whether she continued to want him to or not. And tonight, when she voluntarily took the prescription that was supposed to lead to a cure, he'd never leave her side. Wild horses couldn't drag him away.

For Emma, the anticipation of sleep was anything but comforting. There would be no escape for her if things went as planned. No peaceful rest. No sweet dreams.

Of course, the first instance might have been a fluke, she told herself to buoy her courage. Samantha had explained that just because she'd ostensibly been drugged during her captivity, that didn't mean she was guaranteed to remember when sedated again. Truth to tell, Emma wasn't certain how she felt about trying a second time. If it hadn't been for Sissy, she probably would have waited for her memory to return at its own pace.

"I plan to nap on the sofa," she told Travis and Cleo. "I hope it's not too much of an inconvenience for either of you. I just don't want to actually go to bed."

"Works for me," the older woman said. "I have plenty of knitting to keep me busy until I doze off in my recliner. And Travis can sleep anywhere."

Emma saw him nod. She took off her shoes, pulled the coverlet off the back of the sofa and curled up just as Sissy had earlier. Identifying with the child she loved so dearly, she closed her eyes and turned away so the others wouldn't notice the few silent tears slipping out to dampen her hair at the temple.

Breathing deeply and trying to relax, she was about to give up when she felt the cushions at her feet move and realized Travis had joined her. Knowing he was there, that close, helped tremendously.

She continued to inhale and exhale, drawing oxygen into her lungs and counting the breaths. *Seventeen, eighteen, nineteen...*

Aromas that had been mild and pleasant began to take

*on a rancid air. The jarring beat of a bass in the back-
ground made her teeth ache, her hands clench.*

*Loath to open her eyes and find herself a prisoner, she
was relieved to see she was not. Instead, she was onstage
with the band. The men were supposedly playing while
she sang and Robbie harmonized, but their rendition of
familiar music was truly dreadful.*

*"They're higher than a kite," Robbie had whispered to
her while Jet, Ben and Blake grinned and jumped around,
playing wild, discordant riffs. "What are we going to do?"*

*"Get out of here and leave them to make fools of them-
selves without us," Emma had told her. She picked up Robbie's banjo while the other woman brought the mandolin.*

*"I can't go far. Remember?" Robbie said, hurrying to
keep up.*

"You can't? Why?"

*"Because I'm awaiting trial, of course. I don't know
what I'd do if I couldn't count on you, Emma." She glanced
back at the exit that had led them into the alley behind the
coffeehouse.*

*Shock momentarily stole Emma's voice. "Wait a minute.
Why are you going to be on trial? What about the guys?"*

"I made a plea bargain. They won't be charged."

*"How could you? I mean, what did you have to bargain
except Blake and the others?"*

*"Mack," Robbie said. "He was behind it all, anyway,
and getting a man like him off the streets was more important."*

"Not in my book," Emma argued.

*She set the extra instrument aside as soon as they
reached the steps to the bus where Robbie's little girl slept
peacefully, unaware of the potential loss of her mother.*

*"What about Sissy?" Emma asked. "You can't leave
her. That's crazy. What were you thinking?"*

"It's what I felt I had to do," Robbie insisted. "There's

something else I need to tell you, too. I didn't dare speak a word of it before. Not when we might have been over-heard." Her glance back at the darkened, empty alley was furtive.

Listening closely, Emma held her breath.

Robbie's lips started moving but no sound came out. Emma saw her point to the bus as she spoke, then begin to weep and run up the stairs into the only vehicle the group had managed to hang on to as their unpaid bills had piled up and buried them in debt.

"No!" Emma shouted. "No! Don't go. I didn't hear what you said."

She fought the grasp of unseen hands holding her back, keeping her from following her friend. Robbie was the one person whose support had kept her sane during their band's whirlwind tour and subsequent fall onto hard times.

Darkness flowed over and through Emma as if a ma-levolent force was robbing her of the very essence of life and carrying her deeper into inescapable despair.

"Take care of Sissy," Robbie was calling as if from far, far away. "Use the money to take Sissy and hide until I can come back for her."

Emma finally realized how utterly she had failed. Some-how, Blake must have figured out what his wife had in-tended and had taken steps to thwart her plans. That didn't explain why Robbie hadn't turned him in, too, and thereby escaped going to jail, but a lot more details were begin-ning to make sense.

Emma had evidently been captured before she'd had a chance to flee. Sissy had ended up stuck with a guilty father who didn't deserve her, while innocent Robbie had been carted off to jail. Where was the justice in that?

Caught in a whirlpool of blame and overcome by the realization that she had failed the one person who had *relied upon her completely, Emma covered her face with her hands to stifle sobs of despair.*

Suddenly, she was sinking. Floundering. Reaching out for help and unable to touch the hands of the countless rescuers who were trying to stop her fatal descent into an abyss of guilt and despondency.

A petrifying courtroom scene unfolded. The judge was not only robed all in black, his face was that of a bird of prey. Instead of Robbie, Emma stood before him in shackles. Her crimes were unspeakable. Her culpability evident. There was no one to vouch for her, nobody who was willing to take her part or even listen to her useless explanations.

Nevertheless, she attempted a rebuttal. The judge banged his gavel, silencing her.

Faces of the jurors were masked as they hurled rocks and insults at Emma, hitting her over and over again until she sank to the hard floor.

They were going to kill her for being a poor friend, for failing to rescue an innocent child, and she could not fault them for doing so.

Covering her head with her arms and trying to fend off the blows that kept coming, she waited for the end.

SEVENTEEN

Travis pinned Emma's wrists to keep her from punching him as she lashed out at unseen foes.

"We have to wake her up," Cleo insisted.

"She came out of this by herself the last time," he countered. "I don't know whether it will hurt her to let it go that long again, or not."

"Well, she can't carry on like that for much longer. She's liable to pull a muscle."

"Or I will," he said. "I can't believe how strong she is when she's like this."

"Adrenaline," Cleo offered. "A body can do just about anything when it's scared. Even lift a car off somebody. Unless you're ready to be tossed across the room, you'd best say something to wake her."

Out of logical arguments, he had to agree. "Emma?" His volume increased. "Emma! Wake up."

Although she continued to fight as if her life depended upon it, she did seem to be catching her breath.

Again, more gently, he called, "Emma. Emma, open your eyes. It's Travis. You're safe."

When he saw rapid flickering of her lashes, he was so thankful he almost lost the last smidgen of his tenuous self-control. "Emma? Come back to me, Emma. Please?"

Blinking, she opened her eyes more fully. It took long

seconds for recognition to appear in her wide gaze. As soon as it did, he let go of her wrists.

She apparently realized she'd been weeping because she used the backs of her hands to dash away the tears. Her lips were parted and trembling, her breathing ragged. Little wonder, he mused, since she'd fought her unseen enemies like a tiger.

Cleo leaned closer to present a handful of tissues. "Here, dear. Wipe your face. You're back with us."

"I—I thought…"

"We know," Travis said tenderly. "We watched you dreaming. Can you remember more, now?"

Emma appeared pensive, then pushed herself into a sitting position. "Yes! Yes, I can. Robbie did take the blame because Blake threatened her, but she also named the guy in the fancy Western jacket as the drug supplier. We can probably quit looking for him. He's supposed to have landed in jail, too."

"Good. We have one less enemy to worry about," Travis remarked. "What else?"

He could have sworn he glimpsed a flash of insight that came to her and disappeared in an instant. Frowning, he said, "You did remember more." It was not a question.

"I suppose so. It's just so confusing." Emma pressed the tips of her fingers against her temples. "I saw myself on trial instead of Robbie. I failed her. She asked me to look after Sissy and I acted too slowly. Blake got wind of the plan and locked me up before I could run away with her."

"Where was that? Did you see?"

Emma's brow knit as if she were in pain. "No. Not yet. Maybe the next time…"

"No," Travis said flatly, taking one of her hands and cradling it. "You're not going to put yourself through that again. It's too dangerous."

There was a catch in his voice when he added, "I thought I'd lost you for good, this time."

Emma saw little reason to argue with him. She was in no hurry to return to the torture of her nightmares, either. Since she now knew enough to bait Blake into returning to accost her when she had witnesses, she was satisfied. Sort of.

It did bother her to be keeping a few details from Travis and Cleo, but she rationalized that by reminding herself how she had endangered their lives in the first place. There was no sense compounding the sin by dragging them deeper into her muddled-up plans. If they worked, fine. If they failed, she, alone, would take the fall.

Waiting until Travis and his aunt were settled in their beds and the house had been quiet for over half an hour, Emma sneaked out of her room and tiptoed down the stairs, taking care to avoid the steps that squeaked and hoping Bo's light weight wouldn't affect them as he accompanied her.

She had intended to use the wall-mounted phone in the kitchen until she realized it might make noise. Cleo had left her cell on the counter so Emma chose to borrow it, instead.

A call to the offices of the *Serenity News* resulted in a recorded message. Thankfully, there was an alternate number given for nighttime emergencies.

Hands trembling, Emma jotted down that number and stared at it. She had to find just the right person to write her story—someone who would faithfully report the necessary information without cluttering it up with so much detail it tipped Blake off to her ruse.

She dialed. The call went through. A sleepy, grumpy man barked, "What?"

"Hi. This is Emma Landers. I hate to bother you, but

I'm trying to reach the young woman reporter who asked me for an exclusive story this past Sunday at church. Might you have her number?"

Apparently stubbing his toe or falling over something that banged in the background, the man was muttering when he returned. "It'd better be a real scoop if Marcie expects me to ever do this for her again." He read off a full name and number. "You tell her what I said, you hear?"

"Yes, sir." Emma couldn't help smiling. So far, so good. Now, all she had to do was reach this Marcie and hand her the story on a silver platter. No reporter would turn down a fascinating tale like hers. Not in a million years.

Emma was growing more certain than ever of her success. This plan was going to work. It had to.

She stared out into the night to give herself a moment's respite. It was easy to picture the farmyard and pastures as they appeared in daylight. The rustic beauty of the scene was unforgettable. A memory to be treasured.

So was Travis, she added, sobering and heaving a sigh. By the time all this was over and she'd either succeeded or failed, he would probably hate her for taking matters into her own hands. Nevertheless, she had to handle this her way if she intended to keep him safe. The mere thought of putting that sweet man in more danger made her head ache and her stomach knot. None of this was his fault. He shouldn't have to risk his life because of her mistakes.

But he would, she reasoned. Once Travis heard she was planning to make herself a target in order to lure Blake Browning into committing another crime, he'd either try to thwart her or insist on going along. Neither choice was acceptable. She had gotten herself into this mess and she'd get herself out. Period.

Using the light from the cell phone to see the newest numbers on the scrap of paper, Emma dialed Marcie.

As soon as the young woman answered, Emma started to talk, pausing only occasionally to answer questions.

"Will this appear in the paper soon?" Emma asked.

"A week from Wednesday," Marcie replied, sounding ecstatic. "I wish you'd agreed to talk to me sooner. I've missed today's deadline for new copy and we only go to press once a week. My boss is a real stickler for proper procedure. Hates to bend the rules."

"I gathered as much when I called him to get your number," Emma said, disheartened. "Just do your best. The sooner the better."

"Sure will. And thanks, Ms. Landers. My editor will be speechless when he reads this."

Let's hope he's not the only one, Emma thought, ending the call with a polite goodbye. Travis would be able to see it at the same time Blake did, of course, but by that time her moves would be in play. She'd have left the house and gone for a daily walk in the woods as she'd told the reporter was her habit. Harlan and Adelaide would be standing by to nab Blake as soon as he grabbed her. And they'd be able to arrest him for assault and attempted kidnapping in Arkansas, at the very least.

More than satisfied and so tired she could barely keep her eyes open, she gave Bo a pat on the head and led him upstairs again.

Early next week, as soon as she got the opportunity to make another private call, she'd notify the sheriff's office of her scheme and enlist Harlan's help. She didn't dare tell him too soon or he might try to stop her and ruin everything.

Emma yawned and stretched, then headed for her room. Hopefully, she'd be able to keep Travis—and Cleo—in the dark for that short a time.

Something about Emma's manner had Travis as edgy as a barefoot hunter in a nest of copperheads. All he could imagine was that she had been so traumatized by her last nightmare she had pulled back and become a prisoner of her introspection. Again.

He'd consulted Samantha about his new concerns, of course, and had been assured that Emma's mind simply needed more time to heal itself. That was not good enough for him, yet he knew if he suggested she see a psychologist or psychiatrist she'd go ballistic.

Biding his time and remaining silent about her evident problems was extremely difficult, particularly when he noticed that Bo and the other dogs had begun treating her differently. Did the animals sense the change in her, too? Was that possible?

Sure. Why not? Dogs operated on a different plane than humans did and were instinctively aware of minute alterations in their world. That was what made them good guards, while faithfulness kept them at home.

Watching Bo slink up to Emma with his tail between his legs and his head lowered, Travis had to comment.

"Have you noticed how funny that dog is acting?" he asked her.

She was stroking the hound's broad forehead and scratching behind his pendulous ears while sitting on the top step of the back porch. "Um. Maybe. I hope he's not sick."

Since the old dog and Emma were taking up so much room on the narrow step, Travis leaned a hip against the wooden railing and struck a nonchalant pose. "I think he's okay physically. He just seems depressed."

That brought a chuckle from her and a wag of the hound's tail in response. "Seems to be a lot of that going around," she quipped before sighing deeply. "I'm so worried about Sissy I can hardly stand it."

"The police have been looking for Browning's car.

Around here, it should stand out like a sheep in a herd of Angus cattle."

Emma got to her feet and brushed off her jeans. "That's obviously not enough. It's already been three days since Blake took her."

Travis considered putting his arm around her shoulders to offer comfort, then disregarded the notion. There had been a few times lately when he'd been so certain she needed his moral and physical support he'd offered it without qualms. This was not one of those times.

"I have to make a run to the feed mill this morning," he said, purposely changing the subject. "Is there anything I can get you while I'm in town?"

Seeing her countenance brighten, he had hopes she might actually ask to go with him, although he wasn't sure whether or not he should let her. If she went along, she could be in danger from the men who had been harassing her. If he left her here, with Cleo, the same thing was true. Travis's true dilemma was not where Emma was—it was the fact that he might not be close at hand if she needed him.

"Would you mind picking up a cell phone for me?" she asked. "We'd planned to get one before. With all the confusion at that store, I totally forgot."

"Absolutely," he said, glad to finally have something concrete to do for her.

She was still standing there, so close yet so far. The actual distance between them was mere feet; the emotional distance could have been measured in light-years.

He started to reach for her, meaning only to pat her arm for moral support as any friend might do. Instead, the moment his hand moved she stepped into the embrace he had been yearning for.

Arms slipping around his waist, her cheek resting

against his chest, Emma hugged him tightly. "You're the best, you know that?" she murmured.

It was a pleasure to return her affection. "Hey, if I'd known that promising to buy you something would have brought this on, I'd have done it more often."

When she lifted her gaze to join with his, there were un-shed tears misting her beautiful blue eyes. He raised a hand and cupped her cheek the way he had when he'd first seen the bruise. It and the other physical reminders of her ordeal were nearly gone. Too bad the mental bruises lingered.

"What is it, Emma? What's wrong?" he asked, keeping his tone low while his emotions roiled.

"Everything. Nothing." She spoke so softly he almost couldn't hear her.

"Do you want me to stay with you? I can put off the trip to the feed mill until tomorrow. It's starting to cloud up, anyway, and I don't want to haul sacks of feed in the rain."

"No." Shaking her head, she eased away. "You need to keep taking care of your animals and doing whatever you always do. Cleo and I will be fine while you're gone."

"Harlan has been sending patrol cars by pretty often. It's just that I hate to leave you."

"I've really messed up your life, haven't I?"

That statement and her doe-eyed expression were enough to spur him to lean down and kiss her. He hadn't meant the kiss to be more than a friendly overture, a symbol of forgiveness, yet when he felt her lips softening and trembling beneath his, he was so moved he made it more. Much more.

When she wrapped her arms around his neck and pulled him closer, Travis was lost. What had begun as a chaste kiss deepened into an expression of all the feelings he'd been suppressing, all the pain he'd felt when she'd left him, all the times he'd prayed for the Lord to bring her home.

Breathing unevenly, he cupped her cheeks in both

hands, lifted her face and gazed deeply into her eyes. There was love there. He could see it.

But there was also something more. A sadness, perhaps. An unfulfilled longing that he didn't know how to deal with.

So confused and so in love he could hardly think straight let alone speak coherently, he took a step backward. "I think I'd better get going."

Emma seemed relieved. "I think so, too. Will you be gone long?"

"I don't plan to be. I'm going to Serenity Feed, then to the store for your phone. If the rain holds off I'll stop and see Thad Pearson, too. He took over his brother's business out by the airport."

"I remember the Pearson family. Wasn't Thad a marine?"

"Yes. Since Harlan confiscated my gun, I figured maybe Thad could loan me one."

Emma's eyelids lowered, masking her emotions as she said, "I hope you never need to use it."

"Me, too, but it pays to be prepared."

He pulled her close again to place a brief, parting kiss on her forehead, then released her and reached into his pocket to fist his keys.

As he descended the porch stairs, heading for his farm truck, he wondered if Emma was as in awe of their mutual kiss as he was. Measuring their teenage affection against what they had just shared was akin to comparing a mouse to a lion, a pinch of salt to a ton of sugar.

He'd been right about Emma all along. They did belong together. Somehow, they'd have to figure out a way she could have her career and still be his wife, because she was not going to get away from him again.

Not this time.

Not ever.

EIGHTEEN

"The mail just came," Cleo shouted. "Look what's in the local paper! You're famous."

Emma's heart leaped into her throat and lodged there. It couldn't be. Marcie had sworn they'd been too late to get the story into this edition.

She snatched the newspaper from Cleo and stared at the front page. It was there all right. Every word of it. And she wasn't ready!

"Oh, mercy."

"I know how you must feel," the older woman commiserated, frowning as she scanned the article over Emma's shoulder. "I can't understand how Harlan or Samantha could have let this happen."

Emma knew guilt was written all over her face as she looked up. "They didn't. I did. Only it wasn't supposed to come out until I'd had a chance to brief Harlan and set up a sting."

"A what?" Cleo grabbed her arm. "You're responsible for this?"

"Afraid so. I called the reporter myself. She promised me this couldn't possibly show up in print for another week because we'd missed this week's deadline."

"The story must have really impressed the editor for

him to redo the whole front page at the last minute. So, what're you going to do now?"

"Phone the sheriff's office, for starters. Then keep my head down when Travis sees the paper. I sure hope nobody mentions it while he's in town. I'd rather have a chance to explain myself before he blows his top."

Cleo nodded toward the cell phone lying on the kitchen counter. "Might as well use my phone. I've got more minutes on it than I'll ever use."

"Thanks."

Emma's hands were shaking so badly she could barely dial. Instead of calling 911 when there was no real emergency, she looked up the number of the sheriff's business line and punched it in.

"Sheriff's office. Elaine speaking. How may I direct your call?"

"I need to speak to Harlan. Right now."

"Sorry. He's out. Can I take a message?"

"Then let me talk to Adelaide. This is very important."

"Sorry. She's not here, either. If you'll leave your name and the nature of your business, I'll have one of them get back to you."

"How soon?"

"I have no idea. Sorry."

Frustrated and beginning to fear she was already running out of time, Emma blurted out her dire need to speak to the sheriff or his deputy, left a contact number, then ended the call.

"Nobody home?" Cleo asked.

"No." Emma was staring at the phone in her hand. Desperate to let someone know how much danger she'd be in as soon as Blake and his partner read the newspaper story, she jabbed the emergency numbers.

"Nine-one-one. What's your emergency?"

It was the same woman's voice! "Elaine?"

"That's me. What can I do for you, ma'am?"

"It's Emma Landers again. Isn't there somebody there who can talk to me?"

"Well, normally there would be, but the sheriff and Serenity police were called out to assist the fire department with a wreck on Highway Nine. Besides, you shouldn't call this number if you don't have an emergency. I told you I'd notify them and I will."

"Call them on the radio, then," Emma said. "Please. And tell Harlan to check the front page of today's *News*. I thought I'd have a week to plan everything with him but the reporter gave me bad information. They printed my story too soon. When the man who's been threatening me reads it, he'll come for me. I know he will. Only Harlan won't be there to arrest him if you don't hurry."

"Okay. I'll tell him. In the meantime, if you'll stay on the line I'll be able to relay his reply."

Breathing hard, Emma nodded. She held the phone away and covered the receiver end so she could tell Cleo. "She's going to radio him for me. I'm supposed to hold."

In the yard, the pack of dogs began to bark. Emma could tell from the changes in the direction of the sound that they were running to the front of the house.

As she thrust the cell phone at Cleo, the hackles on Bo's back stood up. "Here," Emma told her. "You listen for me. I'm going to go see who's here. Maybe Harlan was closer than the dispatcher thought."

Although she strongly doubted that assumption, Emma didn't want Cleo exposed to further danger if she could help it. She also didn't want the older woman to be unarmed, so she left the shotgun untouched. Better to face Blake herself, if that's who was here, and try to stall him long enough for official help to arrive.

"Some wonderful plan this is," Emma mumbled. She put out a hand and grasped Bo's collar so he wouldn't dash through the door when she opened it slightly to peek out.

The vehicle in the driveway wasn't a silver sedan. It was a black, dual-tired pickup truck. Jet was behind the wheel and Blake Browning was climbing out the passenger side.

The taste of bile filled her throat. She swallowed hard. Her whole body began to shudder as if the temperature had dropped forty degrees in mere moments.

Bo began a low, menacing growl. The poor old thing was ready to try to defend her, even with half his teeth missing and arthritic joints that made simple walking look as if it caused him discomfort.

"No," Emma told the dog firmly, wedging a knee between him and the barely open door. "You have to stay in the house this time."

The rest of the dogs had taken up strategic positions around the strange truck, barking and circling as if treeing a possum instead of engaging a human target. Only Bo had seemed to understand the degree of danger and Emma refused to allow him to enter the fray.

Staying between the old dog and the opening, she slipped through the door and closed it behind her. Clouds darkened the sky all the way to the horizon, increasing the sensation of dread. Of impending doom. Making her shiver as the temperature plummeted ahead of the storm.

Emma squared her shoulders and demanded, "Where's Sissy?"

"Safe enough. Which is more than I can say for you," Blake replied with a scowl. "You lied to me."

"About what?" *Keep him talking. Stall,* she reminded herself. *Yeah, as if I'd forget to do that.*

"You claimed you had amnesia." He waved a copy of the newspaper. "It says here you remember everything now."

"That may be a slight exaggeration." Emma managed to sound bold in spite of the roiling of her stomach and the sudden weakness in her legs.

"We'll see about that. Get in the truck."

"I think not."

He drew a gun from his jacket pocket and pointed it at her, gesturing with the end of the muzzle. "Think again."

Instinct made her back up until she was pressed against the center of the wooden door. Through it, she thought she heard voices, as if Cleo may have followed with the cell phone.

Please, God, not that, Emma prayed. *Don't let anybody else get hurt because of me.*

She started to edge to one side. Blake motioned to Jet to cut off her avenue of escape while he closed in from the front.

The larger man climbed out of the truck. He, too, brandished a pistol, only his looked like a revolver while Blake's was a small automatic that fit so snugly in his hand it was barely noticeable.

Emma snapped her head from side to side, trying to keep an eye on both men. It was no use. They were getting too far apart.

She saw Jet place his hand on the outside railing at one end of the porch, apparently preparing to leap over it and grab her. In the meantime, Blake was mounting the steps.

Trapped! *Now what?* If she ran from these men they'd either wound her or fell her some other way until they could wring the supposed secret out of her. After that, realistically, they'd probably kill her.

Jet shouted a curse. Emma turned his way just in time to see him whirl and divert his attention. He raised and cocked his gun, preparing to fire at an unseen target.

A boom echoed. Rattled the windows.

Jet hurtled back at the same instant and hit the ground, yowling, rolling and holding his leg.

That was a shotgun blast—at close quarters! Emma realized in a split second. Cleo must have seen what was happening on the porch and circled around to get the drop on their adversaries.

Momentarily stunned, Emma was about to call to Cleo, to warn her about Blake, when he grabbed her from behind with one arm around her neck and jammed his pistol against her temple.

"Stay where you are," Blake shouted, capping the command with colorful curses. "I've got the woman."

He half carried, half dragged Emma to the truck and forced her in the driver's side door, pushing her over to make room for himself and kicking at her tennis shoes with hard, sturdy boots.

In the background, Jet was still howling like a hound dog that had tangled with an angry porcupine.

At least she wouldn't have both men to worry about. Then again, one man with a gun was plenty.

Surely, Cleo would have enough information to report a true emergency to the sheriff, now, Emma reasoned. Unfortunately, there would be no easy ambush and capture if the cops had no idea where Blake was taking her. The plan that had sounded so plausible before was beginning to fall apart at the seams.

And, Emma realized as her spirits plummeted, so was she. Fear was beginning to gain the upper hand over her sense of reason again, and with it came the brain fog that had hampered her so badly before.

No. Not this time, she vowed, gritting her teeth and clenching her fists. She was not going to give in to Blake. Or to her own demons. She'd come this far. This was not the time to meekly surrender or to fold under pressure.

It was the time to stand and fight.

* * *

Travis had come upon the accident on Highway Nine after leaving Pearson Products, so he had stopped to offer assistance. Someone had handed him a road flare and set him to helping direct traffic around the wrecked cars while the paramedics worked to extricate the victims.

Firemen were sweeping broken glass off the road when he got a signal from Harlan.

"You done with me?" Travis asked, jogging up to the sheriff. "I'd like to get home with my load before the rain hits."

"That's why I motioned to you," the portly sheriff said with a grimace. "We've just had a report of a shooting at your place."

Travis's jaw clenched. "When? Who?"

"Simmer down. Your aunt is fine," Harlan assured him. "She put a load of shot into a guy's knee. Says it's the same one we've been looking for. Big and ugly. Name's Jet."

"He's the one who tried to grab Emma when we were in Ash Flat. What was he doing at the house?"

"I take it you haven't seen the *News* today."

"No. Why?"

"There was a tell-all article in it about your Emma. I figured you didn't know about it when I spotted you way out here. I knew you wouldn't have left those women alone if you'd seen the paper."

"What did it say?"

"The important part was that Emma's regained her full memory. The rest was fluff."

"But, she hasn't. She still can't remember some things."

"You sure about that?" Harlan drawled.

"Of course I am. I…" *The recent difference in Emma! Was that why she'd been acting so strangely?*

Travis spun and raced for his truck. Its bed was piled high with sacks of feed but that wouldn't slow him down.

He pushed the accelerator to the floor and spun his tires on the shoulder of the road. When the truck hit pavement, Travis laid rubber for at least fifteen yards.

"I knew I shouldn't have left," he muttered. His hands were gripping the wheel so tightly they ached. At least Harlan had assured him that Cleo was okay. That was something.

A white-hot knot in Travis's stomach began to burn. Cleo was okay. Fine. So why had nobody mentioned Emma other than to cite the newspaper report? What might that mean? Had the sheriff merely forgotten. Or had he, himself, been so overwrought he'd missed hearing everything that was said?

There was one sure way to find out. Travis fumbled his cell phone, knowing he should pull over to make the call yet unwilling to slow down for any reason until he made certain Emma was uninjured.

Cleo answered immediately. "Hello?"

He could tell by the quaver in her usually strong voice that she was terribly upset.

"What happened?"

"Oh, Travis! It was awful. There were two of them. I managed to get one but the other got away."

"It's okay, Aunt Cleo. You did your best."

"No! You don't understand," she shrieked. "Blake was here, too. He—he took Emma!"

If Travis had not been at the wheel of a speeding truck he didn't know what he'd have done. He wanted to shout at the top of his lungs. To fight an unseen enemy. To shut his eyes and deny reality.

He did none of those things. Instead, he demanded, "What was he driving? The same sedan as before?"

"No," Cleo shouted. "He was in a big, black dually."

"Which way was he headed?"

"I don't know I… Out of town. West or south, it looked

like. He'll know all the back roads because he grew up here."

"Yeah, well, so do I. Keep your ears open and your phone handy so you can call me if you hear anything else. Harlan's on his way to you. Will you be okay until he gets there?"

She sounded as if she was pulling herself together pretty well. "You betcha. I've still got the drop on this guy, not that he's about to run off. I nailed him good."

"Keep your distance, anyway, just in case," Travis warned, torn between driving wildly up and down myriad unnamed dirt roads or going back home to wait for word and keep Cleo company.

Sitting back and doing nothing was unthinkable. Even if all he did was burn rubber and waste gas, he had to keep looking. And keep praying he'd locate Emma before it was too late.

Might she actually have remembered more than she'd admitted? If that was the case, perhaps she'd be able to bargain for her life and save herself by giving Browning the clues he sought.

However, Travis reasoned, if Emma had merely been pretending, the time would soon come when she'd be unable to deliver the missing cash and her captor would run out of patience. Blake Browning had never been the sharpest pencil in the box and thanks to the influences of alcohol and drugs, he was probably even less likely to act rationally now.

"I can't lose her. I can't. Even if she turns me down again and goes back to the music business, I have to know she's alive and well."

That was the key, wasn't it? He wished only the best for Emma. Happiness. Fulfillment. The joy of sharing her special gift with the world. Anything beyond that was selfishness on his part.

Silent prayers and fond hopes were all he could manage at this point. He had to find her in time. He simply had to. Failure was unthinkable.

A world without Emma in it was a world where the sun would never again shine.

NINETEEN

The ride in the truck was rough, especially since Blake stuck mostly to dirt roads and the vehicle's suspension was meant for work, not passenger comfort.

Emma had to brace herself to keep from being tossed around in spite of having managed to fasten her seat belt.

Outside, the force of the wind was building, heralding one of the severe storms so typical this time of year. She leaned forward to peer out the windshield. It wouldn't be long before rain started. Rumbles of distant thunder were already loud and the clouds were being lit with lightning from behind, giving them an eerie glow that danced across the sky like strobes manned by erratic giants.

"Where are we going?" Emma dared ask.

Blake sneered. "How about we head for the money you hid and you give it to me." His chuckle sounded raspy, sinister. "Or else."

"It's not in Serenity. You don't think I'd be dumb enough to bring it with me do you?"

"You might be."

Emma was shaking her head forcefully. "No way. Besides, you know what kind of state I was in when I was running from you. I wouldn't have stopped for anything. I was too confused."

"You do have a point," he admitted. "In that case, suppose you tell me where Robbie stashed it?"

"So you won't need me anymore and can kill me?"

"Maybe I'm feeling generous. You wanted the kid. Tell me where the cash is and I'll let you have her."

"No strings attached?"

He snorted derisively. "There are always strings, Emma darlin'. You know that."

"Why should I trust you?"

He laughed again, reminding her of the rowdy way he and the others had behaved when she and Robbie had left them onstage during that frenetic performance.

"You shouldn't," Blake told her. "But it looks to me like you're out of choices."

Although he kept both hands on the steering wheel, he managed to draw her attention to his gun with a brief glance. Emma shivered. The weather wasn't the only thing unsettled and posing a threat, was it? The man beside her was losing what little self-control he had left. Unless the cavalry arrived soon to rescue her, she was probably going to die today.

That thought settled in her heart, astonishingly calming and reassuring. She was a strong enough believer to know where she was going after she drew that final breath. It was the idea of leaving Travis and Sissy behind that devastated her.

Especially Travis, she added, not bothering to argue with herself over that telling conclusion. She loved him more now than ever before and it was her most fervent prayer that he would not blame himself for any of this.

I'm responsible, Emma concluded. *Just me. Nobody else.* By releasing her story to the reporter she had set all this in motion. It hardly mattered that her supposedly perfect plan had backfired. When she'd left Serenity with

Blake and his Browning Brothers band six years ago, she'd started the series of errors that had brought her to this end.

"Everything started to go wrong after I left Travis," she muttered, assuming the noise of the motor and the storm outside the cab of the truck would mask her words.

They did not. Blake's head snapped around. "What did you say?"

"Nothing. I was just talking to myself."

"I don't think so," he countered. A leer showed his ruined teeth. There was perspiration dotting his flushed face and trickling down his forehead.

Emma had seen that reaction before. If he didn't get a fresh fix soon he'd be physically ill. Her spirits rose. Maybe *that* was going to be her deliverance.

Before she had time to plan further, he was easing the truck off the road and onto an even more narrow dirt track. Raindrops the size of quarters were dotting the dusty windshield and running like tears down a dirty face. *Like Sissy's face.*

"Think of your daughter," Emma offered, hoping there was still a smidgen left of the loving father he had once been. "She needs me. I promised Robbie I'd look after Sissy while she was in prison."

"I can take care of my girl."

"Can you? Look at yourself, man. Your hands are shaking and you're sweating like a pig. Until you kick the habit you can't even take care of yourself."

"What do you care? You never liked me, anyway. You just tagged along with the band because you figured we were your ticket to stardom."

Sadly, he was correct. "I was wrong. About a lot of things," she said, nodding. "But I can make amends for some of my bad choices by taking care of Sissy. You know she likes me. She needs a woman's touch. All little girls do."

"Suppose you're right. All you have to do is tell me where Robbie hid the money and I'll let you go."

"Really?" The way Emma saw it, there was about a ten percent chance he'd keep his promises. Maybe even less, given the fact that she was unable to cite specifics about the money. The only information her nightmares had provided was the scene with Robbie, when Emma had been unable to make out what the other woman was trying to tell her before she'd boarded the bus.

Blake seemed to think something was hilariously funny because he began to chortle, then cough before stopping the truck, opening the door and leaning out to be sick.

That was the opportunity Emma needed. She released her seat belt, jerked open the door and slid out.

Hard, incessant rain pelted her, quickly plastering her hair to her cheeks and soaking her clothing. She barely noticed. All she cared about was getting away.

Arkansas clay made the unpaved roadway so slippery she fell repeatedly, caught herself, then kept scrambling forward, not daring to look back.

Blake would surely be behind her. He was larger. Stronger. More dressed for hiking through brush in the middle of a deluge than she was.

She lost her foothold at the edge of a gulley and started to slide backward.

Fingers clawing at the mud, vision blurred by cascading rainwater, Emma grasped handful after handful of rotten leaves and twigs, failing to find a secure hold.

She teetered, her arms windmilling, and almost regained her balance.

Just when she thought she'd make it up the slope, her soggy clothing was grabbed from behind and she was jerked off her feet.

Blake had her. The battle was over. She'd lost.

* * *

As Travis drove aimlessly through territory that was achingly familiar, he wondered if he'd ever see Emma again.

His imagination was working overtime, showing him scenario after scenario—all dreadful. He was about to head for home when his cell rang.

He snatched it up, daring to hope it was good news. "Hello?"

"Travis, it's me," his aunt said. "They've carted Jet off to the hospital. Harlan says for you to come in. There's nothing anybody can do until they spot the truck Blake's driving."

"I know that. I just…"

"Hold on a second."

The silence on the line was more nerve-racking than useless conversation. When Cleo spoke again her voice was muffled, as if she was trying to mask her words.

"Listen up. Adelaide just radioed Harlan. She thinks she's found the truck out near the south fork of the Spring River."

"That covers a lot of ground. Where, exactly?"

"I'll go try to find out."

Travis held his breath. That branch of the Spring did cut through nearby farms and ranches but it also ran for miles, so there was no guarantee the truck was even in Fulton County.

"By Jenkins Ford," Cleo returned to whisper. "Sounds like the place you boys used to go fishin'."

And where Emma and I used to go to be alone and dream about our future, he added to himself. At least they both knew that neck of the woods well enough to keep from getting lost.

"Don't tell Harlan, but I'm close to the ford and heading that way. Thad loaned me a gun."

"Take care," she said. "I'll be prayin' hard that you won't have to use it."

* * *

Parts of the surrounding terrain seemed familiar to Emma as Blake manhandled her through the thick forest, cursing and shoving her whenever she tripped or didn't follow his orders quickly enough to suit him.

"Where are we going?"

"You should know. You were raised here same as me."

Blowing sheets of water blinded her, but at least the rain had helped wash off some of the slimy, red mud. Emma pushed her hair out of her eyes and tried to peer through the stands of budding trees. A glade of dogwoods was the only lightness in sight, their white petals being bombarded by water, their thin branches whipped by the gale.

I'm like them, she thought absently. Smaller and more fragile than others, yet tenacious and flexible enough to bend in the storm to keep from breaking.

A slight smile lifted the corners of her mouth. Those lovely little trees were one of the hidden treasures of the usually plain-looking forest. Every spring, their white flowers appeared in the understory of the larger trees and blinked out at passersby as if delighted to be providing such an unexpected show of loveliness.

Suddenly, Emma's thoughts coalesced and she knew where Blake was taking her. The gulf. A cliff that overlooked the collapsed ceiling of one of the many limestone caves that formed a labyrinth beneath the Ozarks Mountains. Every once in a while, one of the cave roofs would get too thin or too weighed down by stalactites and fall in, leaving a deep pit with unstable rims but spectacular views for those brave enough to creep close to the edge and look down.

She came to such an abrupt halt her captor crashed into her and stepped on her heel. It had not been her intent to leave her shoe behind, but when the mud sucked it off her foot she didn't try to retrieve it. Her feet were already so icy she hardly felt the rough terrain as she continued forward.

They had to be getting close to the unsafe area, she concluded, wondering if either of them would see it in time to keep from falling hundreds of feet onto the jagged formations at the bottom.

Chances of anyone catching up to them at this point were slim and none, Emma realized. Nevertheless, she let herself be herded another hundred yards or so, then surreptitiously shed her other shoe. It wasn't much of a clue, nor was it likely to be spotted when it was covered in so much mud. Still, it gave her the slightest glimmer of hope.

That was all she had left. Hope and faith that someone, someday, would make Blake Browning pay for what he was evidently planning to do to her.

Travis spotted the red-and-blue flashing lights of the patrol car as soon as he turned down the narrow track that led to the river crossing he sought.

Dressed for the foul weather in a slicker, rain pants, rubber boots and a clear, waterproof cover for her hat, Adelaide flagged him down.

"Wait here," she ordered. "Backup's on the way."

Travis did nod but he had no intention of taking orders from anyone, not even Harlan.

"Which way did they go?" he asked as he stepped out into the rain.

"Can't tell. It's too wet. Do you know this area?"

"Yeah. If Emma's leading Blake, I may know where they're headed."

"Suppose he's the one picking the trail?"

"Then your guess is as good as mine," Travis said flatly. "Got another slicker in your car you could loan me?"

"Sorry. No. Just wait in your truck, like I said, and let us handle this."

"I'm the one who's sorry," Travis told her. "I'm not waiting." He saw her hand slip under her coat, ostensibly toward her holster. "You can threaten me all you want. It won't make any difference."

Pausing, he pointed. "Jones Ford is that way. But there's a place Emma and I used to go east of here. That's where I'm headed, so when the others get here, please ask them not to shoot me."

"Travis…"

He could hear her starting to use her radio as he vanished among the trees. Not having the bright yellow slicker was actually an advantage because he'd be virtually invisible in wet, worn denim.

Every few hundred feet he paused just long enough to listen. The worst of the storm had passed so the rain was more steady and the thunder had abated.

Parts of the path he'd taken seemed to have been disturbed recently but he couldn't tell if that was a result of the rushing runoff from the storm or the footsteps of humans.

Torn as to whether he might be on the right track or headed in totally the wrong direction, he was about to turn and backtrack when he saw it. A shoe. A small, once-white tennis shoe.

There was no doubt in his mind that it was Emma's. The question that cut him to the heart was whether she'd been alive when it had dropped off her foot.

Blake took hold of Emma's hair as they approached the precipice of the collapsed cave. She had to grit her teeth to keep from crying out when he yanked her closer.

"All right," he shouted into her ear, his breath so fetid it almost made her gag. "I'm gonna give you one more chance to come clean. Either you tell me where my wife hid the money or over you go. I'm through playing games."

Denial did not seem sensible, even if she didn't know

how to answer his question. Still, she was out of excuses. Now that he'd read the newspaper report, there was no way she'd be able to convince him it was just a ploy. First, he never had believed she'd had amnesia. And second, she had meant her story of recovered memory to sound credible. Too bad it had appeared in print before she'd had time to prepare a defense.

"I—I did remember one thing," Emma sputtered, stalling and wondering if there might be any truth to what she was about to say. "It was weeks after we were all arrested that first time. Robbie told me she'd lied to get the rest of us off the hook with the cops and had made a plea deal that gave up Mack as the big boss."

"Tell me something I don't already know," Blake rasped.

They were both shivering at this point. Emma was merely cold and figured she was suffering from shock. When she saw how badly Blake's hands were shaking and how pale he'd grown, she wondered how much longer he'd be able to stay on his feet. The drugs he'd taken had to be wearing off. Would his collapse come quickly enough to save her?

Struggling for balance, she shrieked when he seemed to be readying to shove her over the edge. Instead, he kept her canted at an awkward angle and demanded, "What else? There must be more."

Was there? There was! "She asked me to take care of Sissy and said there was cash I could take and run away."

"Where!" Blake roared, looking and sounding on the verge of hysteria.

"We—we were standing next to the bus. Robbie pointed to it. But I never had a chance to look for the money because the next thing I knew, you had me locked up in chains."

He blanched and started to relax his grip on her hair.

Emma grabbed his wrist with both hands to keep from toppling into the abyss if he let go too abruptly.

One of her feet started to slip. She could feel the ground passing beneath those toes. As wobbly as Blake was already, they were likely to go over together. The last face she would see was that of her worst enemy.

If only she'd trusted Travis, had told him everything the way she now knew she should have. But she had not. So, she was about to die at the hands of a madman.

A strange peace came over her, as if she were cradled in the arms of God. Emma closed her eyes, weary beyond imagining, summoning her last ounce of strength, nearly through fighting a hopeless battle she could not win.

Wind raced up the steep sides of the chasm, chilling her to the bone. She felt nearly weightless for long seconds, as if she could spread her arms like eagle's wings and ride the updrafts into the clouds.

A strong hand closed around her wrist.

She opened her eyes.

Was she seeing things again? Was her mind playing more tricks?

The agony in Travis's expression told her otherwise. She yearned to reach for him, to move into his embrace and stay there forever.

All three figures on the cliff rim were being buffeted by the gusty remnants of the storm.

Wide-eyed, Emma saw Travis start to falter, to lean too far in her direction.

"Let go!" she screeched at him.

He gritted his teeth and held tight. Sank his heels into the slippery mud and threw himself bodily away from the edge, carrying her with him.

Emma's scream was echoed by another as Blake Browning slid over the edge into oblivion. He managed to get off one wild shot before all was still.

Lying in the mud beside her rescuer, Emma gasped for breath and tried to convince herself Travis was all too real. It wasn't until she saw his unshed tears mixing with rain and felt his arms around her that she truly believed.

Her ordeal was over. They had been given a second chance.

She was still clinging to him and silently weeping for joy when he carried her out of the woods.

He joined her in the waiting sheriff's car where they shared the soggiest, most amazingly wonderful kisses Emma had ever received.

Their trials were finally over.

She smiled at the man she had loved for a long, long time. This wasn't the end.

It was a new beginning.

EPILOGUE

Even without Blake's confession, Emma and Travis were able to provide enough background information to result in a successful appeal of Roberta Browning's conviction.

They'd delayed their wedding day long enough for Robbie to be released and help entertain during and after the ceremony. Logan Malloy, the pastor of Serenity Chapel, was officiating at the outdoor rite while Cleo took charge of the reception to be held later under the shade of spreading oak and sycamore trees.

Sheriff Allgood had managed to locate Emma's mother. She had happily flown back to Arkansas for a reunion and again for the nuptials, ecstatic to learn that her only child was alive and well.

Nervous, Emma accepted her bouquet from Becky Malloy, the pastor's wife. "Did my mom get Sissy dressed okay? She can be difficult sometimes."

"No problem," Becky told her with a wide grin. "Robbie was busy getting her CD accompaniment cued up so I recruited that sweet Jill Andrews to help, too. I figured anybody who'd been Sissy's foster mom for a while would be able to handle anything, even tantrums."

"I hope it doesn't come to that," Emma said with a sigh. "I've tried to explain everything to Sissy but I still don't think she fully gets it."

"She will, in time," the pastor's wife said. "There's no hurry. Now that she has her real mama back she should settle down in a hurry."

"I wish I could say the same for myself. My mom's a sweetie, but she's been hovering so much I had to assign her to look after my flower girl just so I could have a minute's peace."

Emma glanced at herself in the full-length mirror in the upstairs room. "I can't believe I'm actually doing this."

"Getting married, or marrying Travis?"

"Both." Nervous, she giggled. "He insists he's forgiven me for all the problems I caused."

"I'm sure he has." Becky opened the door, looked down and smiled. "I see your escort is ready."

"Hey, don't laugh," Emma said, before doing exactly that. Travis and Cleo had made a lei for Bo that matched her bridal bouquet and had bathed him so well he smelled better than the flowers around his neck.

"Don't you need a leash?" Becky asked.

Emma shook her head. "Nope. He's just like his owner. Faithful and reliable and wants to be sure I'm okay practically every minute. They're both real keepers."

"What about your singing career?"

"If the Lord wants me to find fame He'll bring it to me right here in Serenity," Emma said. "It's taken me a long time, but I've finally realized I didn't have to go anywhere else to fulfill my fondest dreams."

Stepping out into the hall, she gave the faithful hound a pat on his broad head, lifted her chin, smiled and started down the stairs with Bo at her side.

She couldn't wait to be joined to Travis in holy matrimony. For the rest of their lives.

* * * * *

Dear Reader,

Who we are today depends a great deal on who we were yesterday. And yet, nothing is carved in stone. It's possible to turn your life around for the better, particularly by the grace of God.

In the case of Emma Lynn Landers, even though her memories are hazy and her thoughts distorted by trauma, she has not completely lost her identity. Taking steps to return to her roots, to the man she once loved and to the Christian faith that sustains her finally brings peace.

Not all of us can go back the way Emma did, but we can go forward. Yesterday is gone. Today is a gift. Use it wisely.

Thank you for reading *A Trace of Memory.* I hope you enjoyed it!

Blessings,

Valerie Hansen

Questions for Discussion

1. Emma flees without really knowing why she's running away. Have you ever been so overwrought that all you wanted to do was escape? What did you end up doing?

2. Because Emma truly cannot remember what happened to her, she's unable to convince others why she's so frightened. Can you identify with her desire to be believed simply because she's a truthful person?

3. As Emma slowly recalls the events that traumatized her, she's afraid to tell Travis. Is that sensible? Normal?

4. Travis's aunt Cleo is more tolerant of Emma's confusion than Travis is. Is it typical of men to want to fix things, then get upset when they can't?

5. Travis vows to protect Emma no matter what, even if it means keeping her at arm's length. Can you see his motives and appreciate his personal sacrifice?

6. When the criminals harmed Travis's dogs, were you as upset about that as about the harm done to Emma? Have you ever thought of a pet as your best friend?

7. As Emma begins to recover and remember, some of her memories appear as vivid dreams. Do you recall your dreams? Do they ever actually make sense?

8. When Emma finally pictures an innocent child, she gets terribly upset. Have you ever acted because of a

premonition and then found out your instincts were right?

9. When Emma thinks Travis was shot, perhaps fatally, she imagines that the Lord has deserted her. Have you ever felt that kind of hopelessness?

10. Sissy's father tries to use his child to make Emma tell him where a valuable stash of drugs and money is hidden. Can you see why Travis was so against Emma's cooperation until he saw what her plan really was?

11. Travis and Emma manage to communicate to rescue the little girl without a sound. Have you ever felt so in tune with another person that no words were necessary?

12. In the end, Emma has a choice of how to use her God-given talent in the future. Can you understand her decision to "bloom where she's planted?"

REQUEST YOUR FREE BOOKS!

2 FREE RIVETING INSPIRATIONAL NOVELS
PLUS 2 FREE MYSTERY GIFTS

YES! Please send me 2 FREE Love Inspired® Suspense novels and my 2 FREE mystery gifts (gifts are worth about $10). After receiving them, if I don't wish to receive any more books, I can return the shipping statement marked "cancel." If I don't cancel, I will receive 4 brand-new novels every month and be billed just $4.74 per book in the U.S. or $5.24 per book in Canada. That's a savings of at least 21% off the cover price. It's quite a bargain! Shipping and handling is just 50¢ per book in the U.S. and 75¢ per book in Canada.* I understand that accepting the 2 free books and gifts places me under no obligation to buy anything. I can always return a shipment and cancel at any time. Even if I never buy another book, the two free books and gifts are mine to keep forever.

123/323 IDN F5AC

Name _____ (PLEASE PRINT) _____

Address _____ Apt. # _____

City _____ State/Prov. _____ Zip/Postal Code _____

Signature (if under 18, a parent or guardian must sign)

Mail to the Harlequin® Reader Service:
IN U.S.A.: P.O. Box 1867, Buffalo, NY 14240-1867
IN CANADA: P.O. Box 609, Fort Erie, Ontario L2A 5X3

**Are you a current subscriber to Love Inspired Suspense books
and want to receive the larger-print edition?
Call 1-800-873-8635 or visit www.ReaderService.com.**

* Terms and prices subject to change without notice. Prices do not include applicable taxes. Sales tax applicable in N.Y. Canadian residents will be charged applicable taxes. Offer not valid in Quebec. This offer is limited to one order per household. Not valid for current subscribers to Love Inspired Suspense books. All orders subject to credit approval. Credit or debit balances in a customer's account(s) may be offset by any other outstanding balance owed by or to the customer. Please allow 4 to 6 weeks for delivery. Offer available while quantities last.

Your Privacy—The Harlequin® Reader Service is committed to protecting your privacy. Our Privacy Policy is available online at www.ReaderService.com or upon request from the Harlequin Reader Service.
We make a portion of our mailing list available to reputable third parties that offer products we believe may interest you. If you prefer that we not exchange your name with third parties, or if you wish to clarify or modify your communication preferences, please visit us at www.ReaderService.com/consumerchoice or write to us at Harlequin Reader Service Preference Service, P.O. Box 9062, Buffalo, NY 14269. Include your complete name and address.

LIS13R

SPECIAL EXCERPT FROM

Love Inspired
SUSPENSE

*Brave men and women work to protect
the U.S.-Canadian Border.
Read on for a preview of the first book in the new
NORTHERN BORDER PATROL series,
DANGER AT THE BORDER by Terri Reed.*

Biologist Dr. Tessa Cleary shielded her eyes against the late summer sun. She surveyed her surroundings and filled her lungs with the sweet scent of fresh mountain air. Tall conifers dominated the forest, but she detected many deciduous trees as well, which surrounded the sparkling shores of the reservoir lake.

A hidden paradise. One to be enjoyed by those willing to venture to the middle of the Pacific Northwest.

The lake should be filled with boats and swimmers, laughing children, fishing poles and water skis.

But all was still.

Silent.

The seemingly benign water filled with something toxic harming both the wildlife and humans.

Her office had received a distressing call yesterday that dead trout had washed ashore and recreational swimmers were presenting with respiratory distress after swimming in the lake.

As a field biologist for the U.S. Forestry Service Fish and Aquatics Unit, her job was to determine what exactly that "something" was as quickly as possible and stop it.

"Here she is!" a booming voice full of anticipation rang out.

A mixed group of civilians and uniformed personnel gathered on the wide, wooden porch of the ranger station.

All eyes were trained on her. All except one man's.

Tall, with dark hair, he stood in profile talking to the sheriff. Too many people blocked him from full view for her to see an agency logo on his forest-green uniform.

Tessa turned her attention to Ranger Harris. "Do you have any idea where the contamination is originating?"

He shook his head. "We haven't come across the source. At least not on our side of the lake. I'm not sure what's happening across the border." George ran a hand through his graying hair as his gaze strayed to the lake. "Whatever this is, it isn't coming from our side."

"Let's not go casting aspersions on our friends to the north until we know more. Okay, George?"

The deep baritone voice came from Tessa's right. She turned to find herself confronted by a set of midnight-blue eyes. Curiosity lurked in the deep depths of the attractive man towering over her.

Answering curiosity rose within her. Who was he? And why was he here?

For more, pick up DANGER AT THE BORDER.
Available September 2014
wherever Love Inspired books are sold.

Love Inspired

Don't miss a single book in the
BIG SKY CENTENNIAL *miniseries!*
Here's a sneak peek at
HER MONTANA TWINS
by Carolyne Aarsen:

"They're so cute," Brody said.

"Who can't like kittens?" Hannah scooped up another one and held it close, rubbing her nose over the tiny head.

"I meant your kids are cute."

Hannah looked up at him, the kitten still cuddled against her face, appearing surprisingly childlike. Her features were relaxed and she didn't seem as tense as when he'd met her the first time. Her smile dived into his heart. "Well, you're talking to the wrong person about them. I think my kids are adorable, even when they've got chocolate pudding smeared all over their mouths."

He felt a gentle contentment easing into his soul and he wanted to touch her again. To connect with her.

Chrissy patted the kitten and then pushed it away, lurching to her feet.

"Chrissy. Gentle," Hannah admonished her.

"The kitten is fine," Brody said, rescuing the kitten as Chrissy tottered a moment, trying to get her balance on the bunched-up blanket. "Here you go," he said to the mother cat, laying her baby beside her.

Hannah also put her kitten back. She took a moment to stroke Loco's head as if assuring her, then picked up her son and swung him into her arms. "Thanks for taking Corey out on the horse. I know I sounded…irrational, but my reaction was the result of a combination of factors. Ever since the twins were born, I've felt overly protective of them."

"I'm guessing much of that has to do with David's death."

"Partly. Losing David made me realize how fragile life is and, like I told your mother, it also made me feel more vulnerable."

"I wouldn't have done anything to hurt Corey." Brody felt he needed to assure her of that. "You can trust me."

Hannah looked over at him and then gave him a careful smile. "I know that."

Her quiet affirmation created an answering warmth and a faint hope.

Once again he held her gaze. Once again he wanted to touch her. To make a connection beyond the eye contact they seemed to be indulging in over the past few days.

Will Hannah Douglas find love again with handsome
rancher and firefighter Brody Harcourt?
Find out in
HER MONTANA TWINS
by Carolyne Aarsen,
available September 2014 from Love Inspired® Books.

LIEXP0814

Love Inspired®
SUSPENSE
RIVETING INSPIRATIONAL ROMANCE

WILDERNESS TARGET

by

SHARON DUNN

A WANTED WOMAN

Clarissa Jones is running for her life. Though she has no idea why her ex-boss wants her dead, the killers at her heels are very real. Deep in the Montana woods she finds what seems like the perfect hideout in Ezra Fitzgerald's survival training school. The ex-military outdoorsman has the skills and training to keep her safe...but only if she'll lower her defenses enough to let him help. When her attackers close in, Ezra's protection and Clarissa's fierce determination are all that will keep her alive—while the growing bond between them gives her a reason to fight to survive.

Available September 2014
wherever Love Inspired books and ebooks are sold.

Find us on Facebook at
www.Facebook.com/LoveInspiredBooks

LIS44619

Her Hometown Hero

by

Margaret Daley

In a split second, a tragic accident ends Kathleen Somers's ballet career. Her dreams shattered, she returns home to the Soaring S ranch…and her first love. Suddenly the local veterinarian, Dr. Nate Sterling, goes from her ex to her champion. With the help of a lively poodle therapy dog, the cowboy vet sets out to challenge Kathleen's strength and heal her heart. He'll show her there's life beyond dance, even if it means she leaves town again. But maybe, just maybe, he'll convince her there's only one thing in life worth having… and he's standing right in front of her.

Loving and loyal, these dogs mend hearts.

Available September 2014
wherever Love Inspired books and ebooks are sold.

Find us on Facebook at
www.Facebook.com/LoveInspiredBooks

LI87908